TH

A S

CW01024064

The lighted window wa
and he could hear voic
floorboards as someone walked around in the room.

It happened at the very instant he was stepping on to the guttering. There was a loud, hair-raising snarl, and something immensely powerful and heavy leaped up at him from the ground and tore him bodily down from the creeper. His fingers and face were lacerated as the beast's weight dragged him straight through branches and leaves and brought him to the grass with a back-bruising thump. Then the thing rolled on top of him, slavering and snarling and tearing at him with vicious claws. Gene smelled a rank animal odour that was anything but dog, and he screamed in desperation as his sweater was ripped away from his arms, and guzzling jaws bit into his shoulder muscle to tug the flesh away from his collarbone.

Also by Graham Masterton in *Star*

PLAGUE
THE MANITOU
THE DJINN
IKON
THE PARIAH

THE SPHINX

Graham Masterton

A STAR BOOK
published by
the Paperback Division of
W. H. ALLEN & Co. Plc

A Star Book
Published in 1978
by the Paperback Division of
W. H. Allen & Co. Plc
44 Hill Street, London W1X 8LB

Copyright © 1978 by Graham Masterton
Reprinted 1981

Printed and bound in Great Britain by
Anchor Brendon Ltd, Tiptree, Essex

ISBN 0 352 30217 8

This is a work of fiction. All the characters and events portrayed in this book are fictional, and any resemblance to real people or incidents is purely coincidental.

This book is sold subject to the condition that it shall not, by way of trade or otherwise, be lent, resold, hired out or otherwise circulated without the publisher's prior consent in any form of binding or cover other than that in which it is published and without a similar condition including this condition being imposed on the subsequent purchaser.

In memory of
Ross Bristow-Jones

"The fellaheen will tell you of strange, terrible things. The Arabs hate and fear them also, and speak of them by indirection. 'That people,' they call them, nor does one who has traveled in North Africa need ask a second time what the term connotes."

—Seabury Quinn

The Sphinx

One

He could always remember the first time he caught sight of her. Later, he used to joke about it and call it "love at first bite." It was at the Schirra's cocktail party for Henry Ness, the new Secretary of State, to celebrate Henry's inexplicable engagement to that very raucous and very ambitious Caldwell girl. As usual at the Schirra's, there was plenty to drink and nearly as much to eat, and Gene Keiller was right in the middle of talking to a Turkish diplomat with appalling dandruff, simultaneously sinking his teeth into a fresh crab vol-au-vent (he hadn't eaten all day), when the glittering dresses and black tuxedoes parted like the Red Sea and Lorie Semple walked in.

Gene wasn't yet blasé about beautiful women. He hadn't been working for the State Department long enough to get sick to his stomach of all those fawning, crooning, elegant young ladies who cling around the perimeter of Washington society life with no panties on and an unquenchable thirst for any man who might have been mentioned by William F. Buckley, even if it was only once. Gene's immediate boss, Walter Farlowe, had a nose for political groupies and called them the Prone Department. But when Gene looked up with a mouthful of puff pastry and a shred of crab hanging from the side of his chin, he couldn't have cared whether Lorie Semple was a camp-follower or not.

"Hey, Gene," said Senator Hasbaum, leaning over.

"That's one hell of a piece of ass. Take a look at that goddam frontispiece."

Gene nodded, and almost choked. He reached for his napkin, and patted his mouth, and the vol-au-vent went down his throat half-chewed. All he could say was, "Arthur, for once you're damn right."

She didn't seem to have anyone with her. She was tall—taller than every other girl in the room and most of the men. Gene guessed five-foot-eleven, and it turned out later that he was half an inch on the short side. Her height hadn't made her retiring or timid, though. She stalked into the center of the room, under the twinkling chandelier, with a straight, arrogant back and her chin lifted.

"Jesus," whispered Ken Sloane. "Did you ever see a girl who looked like that before?"

Gene said nothing at all. Even the Turkish diplomat, who had been explaining at great and tedious length his absolute commitment to MARV missiles on Turkish soil, couldn't help noticing that Gene was no longer with him and was staring at Lorie Semple like a man who had just seen a religious vision.

"Mr. Keiller," he said, tugging at Gene's sleeve. "Mr. Keiller, we must talk warheads!"

Gene nodded. "You're absolutely right. That's all I can say. You're absolutely damn right."

Lorie Semple had a mane of brushed-back tawny hair that fell over her bare shoulders. Her face was classically beautiful, with a straight nose, a wide and sensual mouth, and upslanted eyes. Around her neck she wore a three-strand choker of emeralds, and nobody in the whole room believed for one moment that they were green glass. She was dressed in a clinging, low backed, empire-line evening dress of flesh-colored silk, so gleaming and tight around the bust that when you first glimpsed her you had to look again, because she looked as if she was topless.

Her breasts were enormous and she obviously wasn't wearing a bra. Her nipples raised the silk into softly shadowed peaks, and when she walked the bouncing of each bosom was enough to quieten conversation and have even the few faithful Washington husbands glancing surreptitiously over their wives' shoulders.

He never knew what impulse really made him do it, but as she stood there, with her straight back and her supercilious look, Gene Keiller stepped forward and held out his hand. It was unnerving, stepping up close, because this tall girl had the kind of green eyes that seem to stare at you heartlessly, like a cat, and Gene had already downed three vodkatinis and wasn't at his best.

"I don't know you," he said, with a lopsided grin.

The girl stared at him. She was at least as tall as he was, and she was wearing some strong, musky perfume that seemed to fill the air around her like a haze.

"I don't know you, either," she replied, in a deep voice that was heavy with some European accent.

"Well," said Gene, "maybe that's a good reason to introduce ourselves!"

The girl stared at him. "Perhaps."

"Only perhaps?"

The girl nodded. "If we don't know each other, perhaps it is better that we remain that way. Strangers."

Gene gave his little diplomatic laugh. "Well, I can see your point. But this is Washington! Everybody has to know everybody around here."

The girl still kept staring at him, almost hypnotically, and the more she stared the more he found himself thrown off his pitch, and shuffling his feet and staring at the carpet. He hadn't felt like this with a girl since he left grade school, and yet here he was, rugged Gene Keiller, with the Florida tan and the wide white smile, the curly-haired Democratic champ who used to kiss all the babies and make Jacksonville housewives swoon with delight, simpering and bumbling worse than Charlie Brown.

"Why?" she said, parting those moist pink lips.

"Er—excuse me? Why what?"

The girl kept staring at him. She didn't seem to blink at all, and that disconcerted him.

"Why does everybody have to know everybody?"

Gene fingered his collar. "Well . . . I guess it's a question of survival. You have to know who your friends are and who your enemies are. It's kind of like the law of the jungle."

"The jungle?"

He smirked. "That's what they say. It's a tough life, you know, being a politician. It doesn't matter how low down the gum tree you happen to be, there's always someone who'd like to climb higher, who'll stand on your head to do it."

"You make it sound . . . very aggressive," she said. He noticed she was wearing earrings made of small curved animals' teeth set in gold. He was gradually managing to overcome his nervousness, but all the same he was conscious that she had the upper hand in this conversation and that all the other guests were watching him out of the corner of their eye and sizing up his performance. He coughed, and waved towards the bar.

"Would you, er, care for a drink?"

She looked at him. There seemed to be long pauses in their conversation, and he got the impression that she was weighing him up with considerable care. *Stalking* him, almost.

"I don't drink," she said simply. "But don't let me stop you. You seem to be enjoying it."

He coughed again. "Well, I, er, like a drink just to unwind. It kind of relaxes the nerves, you know?"

"No," she said, "I don't know. I've never taken a drink in my life."

He blinked at her. "You're kidding! You didn't even raid the cherry brandy in your old woman's kitchen cupboard?"

With a long-fingered, long-nailed hand, she brushed back her tawny hair and shook her head seriously.

"My mother is not an old woman. She is really quite young. And she has never, ever, had alcohol in the house."

"I see," said Gene, embarrassed. "I didn't mean to imply——"

"No, no," she said. "Don't worry. I know what you meant."

For a while, Gene stood there with his empty glass in his hand, giving the girl little smiles and saying "well" and "uh-huh," but not daring to leave her in case any of the other unattached men in the room horned in. There was something about her that frightened him but at the same time was mesmerically fascinating—apart from the fact that she had the biggest pair of tits he had ever seen.

He finally said, "I, er, haven't introduced myself. That's pretty dumb, for a politician! My name's Gene Keiller."

They shook hands. He waited expectantly for the girl to introduce herself, but she said nothing, simply smiled faintly, and kept on looking around the room.

"Aren't you . . . going to . . ."

She turned back and smiled at him.

"Gene Keiller," she said. "I've heard of you."

"Oh, really?" he grinned. "I haven't had too much publicity lately. These days I'm a working politician, not a campaigning one. Promises are one thing, you know, but carrying those promises out is a whole different ballgame."

She nodded. "I thought you were a politician. You talk in such old clichés."

He stared at her. He wasn't sure if he'd heard her correctly, because Senator Hasbaum had just laughed loudly next to his left ear.

"I'm sorry?"

"That's all right," she said, graciously. "All politicians do it. It must be an occupational disease."

He rubbed the back of his neck, which he always did when he was irritated. "Now, wait a minute," he said, in a half-jokey, half-steamed-up kind of voice. "It's all very well for people like you to say that politicians are riddled with clichés, but what you have to remember is that most political situations are——"

"There are none," she said, in that rich voice of hers.

He was about to carry on, but then he looked at her, puzzled. "What?"

"There are no people like me," she said simply.

He frowned, and examined his empty glass again. "Well," he said, "what kind of people are you?"

She stared at him as if she were trying to decide whether he was worthy of such a valuable piece of knowledge. Finally, she said, "I am half-Egyptian and half-French. I am one of those people that are known as Ubasti."

"And is it too much to tell me your name? Or is that a cliché question too?"

She shook her head. "You mustn't let my shyness put you off," she said. "When I am shy, people always seem to think that I am frightening. I can see it in their eyes. Fear and aggressiveness are very similar emotions, don't you think?"

"You still haven't told me your name."

She tilted her head to one side. "Why do you want to know? Do you want to seduce me?"

He looked at her, questioningly. "Do you want to *be* seduced?"

"I don't know. No, I don't think so."

He said bluntly, "You're a very beautiful girl. You know that, don't you?"

She lowered her eyes for the first time since they had started talking. "Beauty is a matter of opinion. I think my breasts are too big."

"I don't think the consensus of American male opinion would agree with you. If you want to know, I think they're stunning."

A hint of color touched her dark-tanned cheeks. She said softly: "I think you are probably saying that to flatter me."

He snorted. "You don't need flattery. You're too good-looking for that. And apart from that, you've got something that every other woman in this whole goddamn room would like to have but never will . . . not in a thousand years."

She looked up. Her green eyes were lambent and fascinating. One moment the pupils seemed to be tight shut, and the next moment they opened out wide like dark flowers.

"You've got mystique," Gene told her. "The moment I laid eyes on you I said to myself, Gene, that girl has mystique. Look at you now—we've been talking all this time and I still don't know your name."

She laughed. The cocktail-party guests standing close by noticed her laughing and Senator Hasbaum whispered to one of his friends, "That Gene Keiller's done it again! By God, I wish I was twenty years younger! I'd show that broad what a Tennessee boy can do!"

The girl said, "Why is my name so important to you?"

Gene shrugged. "What can I call you if I don't know what it is? Supposing I want to ask you to come to dinner with me after the party? How do I say it? 'Excuse me, Ms. X, or Ms. Y, or whatever you call yourself, will you come to dinner with me after the party?' "

She shook her head. "You don't have to say that."

"Then what do I say?"

"Don't say anything, because I can't come."

Gene took her hand, and held it in both his hands.

"Of course you can come. You're not married, are you?"

"No."

"I didn't think you were. You don't have that haunted look that all Washington wives get sooner or later."

"Haunted look?" asked the girl.

"Sure," said Gene. "They're always worrying about which girls their husbands are sleeping with, and whether it's any of the girls that the men *they're* sleeping with have slept with, in which case their husbands may find out they've been sleeping around."

"It sounds complicated."

"You get used to it. It's all part of running a great democracy."

The girl almost unconsciously touched her animal-tooth earring. She said, as if she was thinking of something else, "It doesn't sound . . . very moral."

Gene looked at her cautiously. "Moral" was a word he hadn't heard in a long time, not since he'd made his reputation four years ago down south by exposing a swamp-draining scheme for the money-grubbing scandal it was. On this girl's lips it sounded curious, out of place. Here she was, at a Washington cocktail party, dressed in skin-tight, flesh-colored silk, with the most eye-stopping figure since Dolly Parton, and she was talking about *morality*.

"Listen," he said gently. "This life is full of stresses and strains. For many people, many politicians, fooling around is the only recreation they get."

"I'm sorry," said the girl. "Fooling around is not *my* recreation."

Gene spread his hands wide in apology. "Okay. I didn't mean to suggest anything. I think you're a beautiful girl, and I'd be some kind of monk if I didn't find you sexy. Now, wouldn't I?"

She blinked at him in bewilderment. "You . . . find me . . . sexy?"

Gene almost laughed. "Well, of course I damn well do! What the hell were you thinking about when you put that dress on this evening?"

She blushed. "I don't know. I didn't think . . ."

Gene took her hand again. "Honey," he said, "I think you'd better tell me your name. It's going to make life a lot easier."

"All right. I'm Lorie Semple."

Gene frowned. "Semple? Wasn't your father——"

"Jean Semple, yes, the French diplomat."

Gene squeezed her fingers gently. "I was sorry to hear about that. I never met him, but a few of my friends said he was a terrific guy. I'm sorry."

"You don't have to be. He always knew that he was living dangerously. My mother says that he is probably more fulfilled now than he ever was."

Gene managed to catch the sleeve of a passing

waiter, and say "vodkatini" before the man dashed off. Then he turned back to Lorie.

"Are you sure I can't persuade you to come and have dinner? I've been meaning to test my teeth on the *gigot* at the Montpellier for months."

She shook her head. "I'm sorry, Gene."

"I don't understand why," he said. "I may not be Rock Hudson, but I'm still pretty chunky. Chunky guys like me are hard to find in politics. You want to go out with bespectacled weeds from the Treasury all your life?"

"Gene," she said, and he caught the strong scent of her perfume, "I don't meant to be rude. I don't want to hurt your feelings, either. But I came because my father was invited here before he died, and I thought it would be polite. Once I have said all the right things to all the right people, I must go."

"You're not wearing black," he said, quite suddenly.

"No," she said. "In my family, for generations, the death of the male has been regarded as—well, a cause for celebration. I am celebrating because my father has fulfilled his duty in this world, and is now at peace."

"You're *celebrating*?" Gene asked.

Lorie lifted her head to stare straight into his eyes. "It is the way of our kind. It is the way we are. It is the way we have always been."

Gene was still trying to work this out when the waiter brought his drink. He tipped the man a dollar, and then said unsteadily, "Lorie, I don't mean to pry, but I've never met a family that celebrates death before."

She turned away. "I shouldn't have mentioned it. I know it shocks some people. We just feel that when a man's life is over, he has finished his work, and that in itself is cause for pleasure."

"Well, I'll be damned," he said, and sipped his ice-cold drink.

Lorie turned. "I have to leave now."

"Already? You've only been here a few minutes. This bash is going to go on till three. You wait till Mrs. Marowsky starts her stripping act. Once you've seen that, anything you ever thought about morality is going to go *right* out of the window."

"Don't mock me, Gene," Lorie said.

"Honey, I'm not mocking you. I just don't want you to go."

"I know. I'm sorry. But I have to."

Quietly, impossibly, as if he had been materialized by *Star Trek* tele-transportation beam, a tall, swarthy man in a black chauffeur's uniform appeared at Lorie's side. He had a black beard, trimmed with obsessive neatness, and he wore black leather gloves. He said nothing, but stood just behind her, his hard expression giving Gene no doubts at all that it was going-home time, friends, and anyone who thought otherwise could lump it. He could have been an Arab, or a Turk, but whatever he was he was silent and hard and protective, and Lorie Semple retreated into his protectiveness at once.

"Goodbye, Mr. Keiller. It's been good to meet you."

"Lorie——"

"Really, I have to go now. Mother will be expecting me."

"Well, let me drive you home. That's the least I can do."

"It's quite all right. This is my chauffeur. Please don't bother."

"Lorie, I *insist*. I'm a hot-shot politician at the Department of State, and I absolutely insist."

Lorie bit her lip. She turned to the hard-faced chauffeur standing beside her and said, "Could I?"

There was a long silence. Gene was aware that Senator Hasbaum and several other friends of his were watching, but he was too busy with this extraordinary relationship between Lorie and her silent chauffeur to worry about them. He looked evenly and confidently at the chauffeur, and in his turn, the chauffeur scrutinized him.

Finally, the chauffeur nodded. It was an auction-bidder's nod, almost imperceptible if you weren't watching for it. Lorie smiled, and said, "Thank you, Gene. I'd love to."

"That's the first sensible thing you've said all evening." Gene said. "Just give me a minute to say goodbye to the Secretary."

Lorie nodded. "All right. I'll see you outside."

Gene winked at Senator Hasbaum as he pushed his way through the cocktail guests to find Henry Ness. As usual, the young and dynamic Secretary of State was surrounded by a crowd of women, burbling like doves in a dovecot over every platitude that fell from his lips. His new fiancée, Reta Caldwell, was clinging on to his arm in a ruby-red evening dress that made her bulge out in all the wrong places, and it would have taken bolt-cutters to get her away.

"Henry," called Gene. "Hey, Henry!"

Henry Ness turned around, his smooth Clark Kent face fixed in the confident smile that experienced politicians automatically stick on their faces when anybody says "Hey!" It could, after all, be a photographer, and after Nixon's notorious scowls there was a kind of frenetic nervousness in the Democratic camp that everyone should always look joyful.

"Gene, how are you?" said Ness. He reached over the head of a diminutive woman and shook hands. "I hear good reports of your Mexican file."

"Well, it's shaping up fine," said Gene. "But I guess you're shaping up better. Congratulations on your engagement, Henry. You too, Reta. You're looking swell."

Reta glared at him. He had known her before, years ago, when he was a young and inexperienced campaigner on the State assembly circuit, and she probably remembered that he had seen her paralytically drunk at a campaign party, slobbering kisses over acutely embarrassed party chiefs.

"Henry, I have to leave now," said Gene. "Pressures of state—you know how it is. But truly, Henry, all my best wishes for the future. I hope you're both going to be very happy."

Henry shook his hand again, smiled unconvincingly, and then turned warmly back to his swooning audience of Washington ladies. Henry liked talking to women, Gene considered, as he elbowed his way out of the party toward the door. They didn't answer back, and they didn't ask awkward questions like what the hell are we going to do about multiple-warhead missiles on Turkish soil, and are we going to let the Communists continue to infiltrate black Africa unchecked? All women wanted to know was what he wore in bed, or preferably what he didn't.

Gene collected his raincoat and walked across the polished marble hallway of the Schirra's grandiose house toward the open front doors. It had stopped raining, but the streets and the sidewalks were still wet, and there was a warm breeze blowing that promised more showers before the night was out. Lorie and her chauffeur were standing on the steps, and as Gene came nearer, it seemed that she was leaning close to the chauffeur's ear and whispering something. Gene hesitated for a moment, but then Lorie turned and saw him and smiled. Without a word, the chauffeur left her side and went down the steps to collect his car, a glossy black Fleetwood limousine with a coaching lamp on the roof. He climbed into it, and waited at the curb with the motor idling—not once looking their way, but as watchful and protective as a fierce dog.

Lorie tied a long red velvet cape around her shoulders and brushed back her hair with her hand. "I think my chauffeur's nervous," she grinned. "Mother told him to keep an eye on me, and he doesn't like to let me out of his sight."

Gene took Lorie's hand. "Is he always as cagey as that?" he asked her. "I get the feeling that if I nibbled your ear, he'd be out of that car and beating me into a pulp before I could say 'goodbye, Capitol Hill.' "

Lorie laughed. "He's very good at his job. Mother says he's the most conscientious servant she's had for years. He's an expert in kravmaga."

"Kravmaga? What the hell's that?"

"It's a kind of self-defense thing, like kung-fu. I think the Israelis invented it. You totally dedicate yourself to the destruction of your opponent by whatever means possible."

Gene raised his eyebrows. "It sounds like a slightly less hypocritical version of politics."

They stood on the rainy sidewalk waiting for Gene's car to come around from the car park. A footman in yellow livery shuffled around beside them, surreptitiously smoking a cigarette. A few hundred yards away, across the grass, the illuminated spire of the Washington Monument rose like a spectral tombstone in the damp evening air. A siren warbled somewhere over on M Street.

"You mustn't blame Mathieu for doing his job," Lorie said.

"Mathieu? That's your chauffeur?"

"He's mute, you know. He can't speak a word. He worked for the French secret service in Algeria, and the rebels tugged out all his fingernails and cut out his tongue."

"You're kidding."

"No, it's true."

Gene turned his head and looked for a long and thoughtful moment at the black Cadillac, still idling quietly by the curb nearby. In the driving mirror he could see Mathieu's eyes, hard and watchful, as if they were floating by themselves in the air.

"A thing like that—it must make a guy kind of edgy."

Lorie nodded. "I suppose so. Is this your car?"

Gene's white New Yorker was pulled up to the curb, and the footman opened the doors for them. Gene pressed a dollar into the discreetly placed palms of both footman and carhop and then settled himself down behind the steering wheel.

"Do you want to direct me?" he asked Lorie.

Lorie shook her head. "Mathieu will drive on ahead. All you have to do is follow him."

"No detours?"

"Not unless you want him chasing after us. And I can assure you, he won't let us get away."

Gene pulled away from the curb, traffic signals flashing. "Doesn't that ever bother you? Being kept on a tight rein like that? You're a grown-up girl now."

She released the catch of her cape and let it fall back from her shoulders. In the flickering light of passing streetlamps, he could see the shine on her lips, the intense green sparkle of her emerald choker, and the sheen of silk on her breasts. Inside the car, that musky perfume of hers seemed even stronger, and for a girl who professed to be so quiet and so moral it seemed peculiarly rampant and aggressive. For some reason it reminded him of an animal in heat.

"I suppose you find us strange," said Lorie huskily. "But you must remember that we're not Americans. This is not our country. That's why we stay close together and guard each other. Apart from that . . ."

"Apart from that, what?"

She lowered her eyes. "Well, we're different, I suppose. And when you're different, you tend to keep your own company."

Ahead of them, the red taillights of Mathieu's limousine turned left, and Gene followed. It was starting to rain again, and a few drops spattered the windshield. Gene switched on the wipers.

"Can I ask you something?" he said to Lorie.

She nodded. "As long as it's not too personal."

"Well, I guess it is kind of personal, and you don't have to answer if you don't want to but it's the sort of question that a guy always thinks about when he meets a girl as beautiful as you."

"You're flattering me again."

"Damn it, I'm paying you a compliment! Don't people ever pay you compliments? Hasn't a man ever said that to you before?"

She shook her head.

"Anyway," he said, "that was my question. I wanted to know if you had a steady boyfriend. Anyone in tow. I wanted to know if you were tied up with someone, some man, or whether you were free."

Lorie looked away. "Does it matter?" she said.

Gene shrugged. "Well, I don't know. It matters to some girls. If they're going steady with someone, they won't contemplate the possibility of anyone else.

There's still some loyalty left in the world, although you wouldn't believe it."

She said nothing for a long while, and even when Gene glanced across at her, she didn't turn or smile.

Eventually, as they were driving past the Watergate, she said softly, "There aren't any men. None at all."

"None?" he said, surprised. "Not even an aged admirer who pesters you with dinner invitations and buys you emerald chokers?"

She touched the jewels around her neck. "Nobody bought this. It's a family heirloom. And no, there are no old admirers. Not even any young admirers."

The way she said that made him frown at her in disbelief.

"Are you saying you haven't any boyfriends at all?"

"Not only now, Gene, but never."

He looked ahead at the road, and the glowing rear lights of Mathieu's limousine. He found it completely incredible that a girl with Lorie's looks and figure should never have dated a boy. He guessed her age at nineteen or twenty, and most Washington groupies by that age had lain on their backs for half a government department, as well as a minor galaxy of congressmen and senators. He knew she wasn't a groupie, but even the nicest girl from the nicest family gets to date *one* boy, even if he's only a carefully selected Harvard frattie.

"You're a virgin?" he asked.

She lifted her chin and looked at him, and he caught the same aloof self-possession in her eyes that he had seen when she first walked into the Schirra's party.

"If that's what you want to call it," she said.

He was flustered. "I didn't mean to call it anything. It just kind of surprised me."

"Is it so rare these days, for an unmarried girl to be pure?"

He pulled a face. "Well . . . yes, I guess it is. Somehow you don't expect it. It's just that . . . well, you don't . . ."

"I don't *look* like a virgin?"

"I didn't say that."

"You didn't have to. You've been telling me how sexy you think I am from the moment you first said hello. If you think I'm sexy, you must think I sleep with men."

"That's not true at all. When I say you're sexy, I mean that you have a direct sensual effect on me personally. When I look at you, when I'm near you, I'm sexually aroused. Now, that's a compliment, not an insult, and I wish you'd take it for what it is."

Lorie said nothing. He thought at first that he'd successfully offended her, but when he glanced across at her again he saw that she was sitting there with a tiny, amused smile on her face.

"Jesus Christ," he said, "you're the strangest girl I ever met. And I've met some strange ones."

She laughed. Then she pointed ahead to Mathieu's car and said, "You'd better watch the road. We're almost there."

They were four or five miles out of the city center now, in a leafy and expensive suburb of ante-bellum houses with pillared porches and white-painted shutters. Mathieu turned off at a narrow, winding side road that led them upward through a tunnel of overhanging trees, and soon they were driving alongside a high wall of mature brick, overgrown with moss and creepers and topped with rows of long, rusty spikes.

"That's the wall of our garden," said Lorie. "The house is just around here."

They turned a sharp corner, and then Mathieu's brake lights glared. They stopped. They were parked in a semi-circular driveway that led up to a pair of high wrought-iron gates. Beyond the gates Gene could see a freshly graveled, private road that led away into the gloom, but the house was obviously set too far back to be seen from the road.

Mathieu didn't leave his car, but sat there with his engine still turning over, watching them in his rear-view mirror. The plume of exhaust rose from the back of his limousine into the rainy night.

"Is this the end of the line? Chez Semple?" Gene asked.

"That's right," Lorie said, tying up the string of her cape.

"You mean I just drop you here and that's it?"

She looked at him with those green, feline eyes. "What did you expect? You offered to drive me home, and now you've driven me home."

"I don't even get invited in for a mug of Ovaltine?"

She shook her head. "I'm sorry. I'd like to, but mother hasn't been too well."

"I'm not going to ask *her* to make it."

"Make what?"

"The Ovaltine, of course. She can stay in bed if she likes."

Lorie reached out and touched the back of his hand.

"Gene," she said, "you're very sweet, and I like you——"

"But you're not going to invite me in. All right, I get the picture."

"It's not that."

He raised his hands in mock-surrender. "I know what it is and what it isn't," he said. "You're a lovely young girl with a close-knit family, and you've always done everything with Momma's approval, in the right, old-fashioned way. Well, suppose I said that's all right by me."

"Meaning?"

"Meaning I'll call on you tomorrow at some respectable hour, present myself to your mother, and ask if I can take you out for lunch. I will even undertake to return you, unraped, before dusk."

She stared at him for a long moment, and then slowly shook her head.

"Gene," she said, "it's impossible."

"What's impossible about lunch?"

She turned away. "I like you," she said. "*That's* what's impossible about lunch."

"You like me, so you won't go out with me? What kind of logic is that?"

She opened the door of the car. "Gene," she said softly, "I really think it's better if you just forget you ever met me. Please—for your own sake. I don't want you to get hurt."

Gene rubbed his neck in exasperation. "Lorie," he told her, "I'm really old enough to look after myself. I may not be an expert in Israeli kung-fu, but I've been through enough emotional experiences to have a certain protective coating of scar tissue. If I backed away from every potential relationship just because I thought I was going to get hurt—Jesus, I'd end up a virgin, just like you."

"Gene, please."

"It's all very well saying 'please' like that, but I don't understand. If you find me incredibly ugly and objectionable, I could follow your thinking, but it's pretty plain that you don't. I've driven you home. I've told you I think you're beautiful. Don't I even deserve an explanation?"

She didn't answer at first. One side of her face was lit red by the light of Mathieu's taillights, and the other side was in shadow. Gene was uncomfortably reminded of Mathieu's constant observation by the ceaseless drone of the Cadillac's eight-liter engine. In some way that he couldn't grasp, he felt extremely defenseless and open to danger, as if this curious situation was suddenly going to turn nasty.

"Gene," whispered Lorie. "I'm going."

She started to climb out of the car, but he reached out and held her wrist. For a split second, she tugged away from him with a strength that almost had him him off-balance, but then she abruptly relaxed, as if by conscious effort, and allowed him to pull her gently back into the passenger seat.

He reached over and kissed her. Her lips were very soft and moist against his, but she wouldn't open them. He held her closer, trying to push the tip of his tongue into her mouth, but she held her head back stiffly and wouldn't let him. She didn't seem to resist as long as he was happy with a junior-high-school, lips-closed kiss, but with a girl as sensual as Lorie, he found that the sheer frustration of it was almost more than he could take.

His left hand touched her shoulder. With his mouth against hers, she tried to push him away, said "mmmm-mmmmhhh," and wriggled. For one brief tantalizing moment, his fingers caressed her breast, heavy and taut and warm, but then he felt a sharp bite on his tongue, and she twisted away from him, and climbed awkwardly out of the car.

He dabbed his mouth with his fingers. There was blood on them, and he felt the sickly taste of it running down his throat. He took his clean white handkerchief out of his breast pocket, and held it against his lips.

Lorie stood there, anxious and frowning, but he didn't look up at her at all. *Christ! Bitten by a goddamn high-school virgin!* He didn't know who made him angrier—Lorie for making a midnight snack out of his tongue, or himself for trying to kiss a broad who actually professed to have morals.

"Gene . . ."

He still didn't look up.

"Gene, I'm sorry, you didn't leave me any choice."

He coughed, and spat some blood into his handkerchief. "Just go home to your mother, will you?" he mumbled.

"Gene, you have to understand that it wouldn't work. Not in a thousand years."

"You bet your ass it wouldn't work! If I want to get eaten alive, I can go back to the Everglades and lay down in front of an alligator!"

"Please, Gene. Don't you see that I like you?"

He tested the flow of blood. It seemed to be easing up now, but she had certainly given him a deep and vicious bite. He had nearly ended up joining Mathieu in the tongueless brigade, and that certainly wouldn't have helped his political ambitions very much.

"Just get out of here, will you?" he said. "I'm going home."

Mathieu had left his limousine and now stood a few yards away, watching Lorie silently and impassively. Another shower had started, and the rain was making a soft, prickling noise on the gravel and the grass.

Lorie finally turned and walked away. Mathieu took her arm, and ushered her over to the Cadillac. As he opened the rear door for her, he looked back at Gene with a face as emotionless as a manhole cover in the road. Then he climbed into the car himself and drove toward the wrought-iron gates.

In utter silence, as the limousine approached, the gates swung open. Then, after it had passed, they swung closed again, and locked. Gene saw the car's red lights disappearing down the gravel driveway, flickering past trees and bushes until they were out of sight. After that, there was nothing but the high forbidding wall, the closed gates, and the rain that sprinkled the grass.

He sat there for a while, and then he switched his car engine off. Still holding the handkerchief to his tongue, he opened his door and stepped out into the rain. Out here, it was so far away from the streetlights of the city that he could see dim clouds passing overhead and a faint moon shining above the trees.

He walked as quietly as he could toward the gates. He didn't want to touch them, in case they were electrified, but he stood as close as he could and peered through. The driveway led down a long avenue of oak trees and disappeared about five hundred yards away around a bend, which presumably led up to the main house. He thought he could see the dark silhouette of a roof and chimneys, but it may just have been the branches of the trees.

There was something sinister and yet intriguing about the Semple house. He wanted to have a glimpse of it, even if only to satisfy himself that it was just another expensive diplomatic mansion with the coach lamps, the rosemary bushes, and all the usual trimmings. He went back to his car, leaned in to open the glove box, and took out the small set of screwdrivers that one of his girlfriends had given him with the attached message "from your favorite screw, with love."

One of the screwdrivers was a bulb-tester. He took it out, and walked cautiously back to the wrought-iron gates. Then, very gingerly, he reached out with the metal tip of the screwdriver and touched one of the iron curlicues. Nothing happened. The gate wasn't electrified, after all. He looked up at it. It was so high, and spiked with such long and barbaric spears, that it probably didn't need to be. The thought of being impaled on one of those made his groin feel distinctly odd.

He grasped the gates with both hands, and then found a foothold. It wasn't difficult to climb up the first six feet or so, because there were plenty of scrolls and leaves to hang on to, and even though he was breathing hard from the exertion, he was able to get up there in only a few seconds. Higher up, it was more difficult. There were fewer curls of iron, and at the very top there were nothing but upright spears, with points that were rusted into vicious sharpness.

He stopped to rest for a moment about ten feet up. Looking behind him, he could see his white car with its doors still open, and beyond that the darkness of the road that led up to the Semple house and the distant gleam of a few neighboring lights. In front, through the prison-like bars of the gate, he could still see nothing more than gloomy overhanging trees, and the pale ribbon of the driveway leading between them. The rain had eased off now, and there was a light, fresh breeze. He wished his tongue wasn't so damned sore, but then that was partly the reason he was halfway up this Gothic gate.

"Upward, my boy, ever upward," he breathed to himself, quoting the long-ago words of his campaign agent in Florida. He gripped two of the iron spear-shafts, pressed the soles of both his shoes against the gate, and began to hoist himself further up like a Fiji islander scaling a coconut tree.

Panting, he reached the top. The tricky bit was going to be climbing over the spikes themselves. There was no foothold, and he would have to try to wedge his feet in between the uprights and hope that they didn't slip or, even worse, get irrevocably stuck.

He jammed his left foot in, and carefully swung his right leg over the spikes. The gates rattled a little under his weight. He stayed there, taking deep breaths, until he could summon up the strength to wedge his right foot in between the shafts on the other side and swing his left leg over.

Just then, he heard a deep rumbling noise from the direction of the house. He froze, sweat trickling down the sides of his face, and listened. It was probably nothing more than distant thunder. There was a warning of electric storms overnight, and they usually rolled into Washington from this side of the river. He gripped the gates tighter, and prepared to hop over.

The rumbling came again, and this time it definitely wasn't thunder. It could have been a motorcycle, or a jet airplane, but it definitely wasn't thunder. He squinted into the Semple grounds through the darkness, but a bank of clouds had obscured the moon and it was impossible to make anything out but shadowy trees. The rumbling was certainly coming from there.

Then he heard the most frightening sound he had ever heard in his life. It was the bounding, rustling noise of large animals running through the bushes and trees. What's more, they were coming his way. *The Semples had set their dogs on him!*

Tense and terrified, he swung his leg back over the top of the gate. The running noise was coming nearer, and he didn't dare to look toward the house. He struggled to extricate his left foot from between the spear-shafts, but because he was off-balance it wouldn't come out. He wrenched it as hard as he could, but it was still stuck.

He was aware of huge, pale shapes leaping through the oaks and the undergrowth, and the scuff of heavy paws on gravel. Then he lost his grip, and half-slithered, half-dropped off the gate to the ground, twisting his ankle and leaving his left shoe still wedged between the bars.

Gasping in pain, he limped towards his car as fast as he could. Just behind him, he heard the rattling thump and scratching of the Semple's beasts as they reached the gates and threw themselves up at them, snarling and growling in frustrated aggression.

He started the car, swung it around in a slew of gravel, and headed back down the winding hill with screeching tires. It was only when he was back on the main highway toward Washington that he slowed down and allowed himself to breathe normally. His whole system felt swamped with fear and hyped with adrenalin.

He reached his apartment in Georgetown and left the car parked in the street. It was a quiet, old neighborhood, and he had been lucky to rent the top floor of a dark, brick house that was set back in its own paved yard. The owner was a friend of his father from the days when students wore coonskin coats and thought that Artie Shaw was the bee's knees. He swung open the gate and limped on his sprained, stockinged foot to the front door.

He switched on all the lamps in his pale-yellow decorated sitting-room, turned on the late-night movie with no volume, and put Mozart's string quartets on the quad stereo. Only then did he permit his brain to start thinking about Lorie Semple. He splashed himself a large glass of Jack Daniels and lay back on the gold-upholstered couch with his injured foot on the onyx coffee-table, turning over the night's events and trying to make something out of them that didn't seem ludicrous or bizarre.

There was no question that Lorie was a fascinating girl. In normal circumstances, he would have expected to be having dinner with her right now, with a promise of bed in her eyes and the orchestra playing seductive music. He would at least have expected to come away from it all with a date fixed for tomorrow. But she was stonewalling him cold, even though she claimed that she liked him, and she was even prepared to bite him to make herself understood.

He lit a cigarette, and suddenly realized how sore his tongue was. He went through to the small brown-and-black bathroom, with its serried ranks of expensive bottles of aftershave, and switched on the light over the wash-basin mirror. Then he stuck his tongue out and inspected it.

The strange thing was that the scarlet wounds were so few and far between. A normal human bite is even and crescent-shaped, but this one consisted of only four distinct marks. Gene touched them gently, and winced. It was almost as if he had been bitten on the tongue by a large dog.

He stood in front of the mirror a long time, and when the phone rang he jumped in nervous surprise.

Two

It was Walter Farlowe, his boss. He wanted to remind Gene that there was an eleven o'clock meeting the following day to discuss the West Indies negotiations, and that he expected Gene's punctual attendance. Gene said he had everything ready, and that everything was fine.

"Do you have a headcold?" asked Walter.

"Do I sound as if I do?"

"I don't know. You sound funny. Like your mouth is full of breadroll or something."

"Oh, that," said Gene. "I bit my tongue by mistake."

Walter chuckled. "You bit your tongue? I wish Henry Ness would."

"I wish Henry would bite his whole goddamned head off."

After putting the phone down, Gene poured himself another drink and sat down to think some more. All his political life he had made his mark by being the kind of man who finishes everything he sets out to do. Every file, every report, every incident was carefully documented, detailed, and closed. Loose ends disturbed him, and that was exactly what this business with Lorie Semple had turned out to be. Apart from that, his pride had taken its biggest beating in twenty years. Not only had a busty nineteen-year-old virgin bitten his tongue, but she'd set her watchdogs on him and made him leave one of his $75 English shoes stuck in a goddamn gate.

He groped around for his telephone book and looked up the Semples. As he expected, they weren't listed. He stood there tapping his glass thoughtfully against his front teeth for a while, and then he picked up the phone and dialed a number. After all, he thought, it's only just past midnight, and not many young ladies in Washington go to bed this early to sleep.

The phone rang ten or eleven times before it was answered. A dozey girl's voice said, "Hello? Who is this?"

"Maggie," said Gene, as brightly as he could manage. "It's me, Gene."

"What's the time?"

"Oh, I don't know. Around twelve I guess."

"You don't know? I buy you a three-hundred-dollar Jaeger-le-Coultre and you don't know?"

"Don't get sore. You weren't asleep, were you?"

Maggie let out a long, patient sigh. "No, Gene, I wasn't asleep. How could any girl keep a job as your private secretary if she ever slept? I am awake, twenty four hours of the day. It's just that some of the time I'm a little less awake than the rest of the time."

Gene listened patiently. "Maggie," he said. "I know this is kind of an imposition, but I was wondering if you could do me a small favor."

"That's what you always say. Gene, it's my night off! Just for once, can't a girl get some of that rest that makes her beautiful?"

"Maggie, you're always beautiful, rested or exhausted."

"Don't give me that. What do you want me to do?"

"Do you remember a French diplomat called Jean

Semple? He died about three months ago in Canada or someplace."

"That's right. He was mauled by bears on a hunting trip."

"Well, what do you know about his background? His family? Particularly his house?"

"Nothing at all. Why?"

Gene picked up the phone and walked over to the couch. On the color TV screen, some moth-eaten monsters were rising from their graves, and a bunch of terrified people were running away, waving their arms in the air, and mouthing silently. Mozart continued to play calmly in the background.

"I met Semple's daughter tonight, 'round at the Schirra's. She was very mysterious, you know? Very . . . what can I say? . . . remote. I get the feeling there's something strange about her that I ought to know."

Maggie sighed again. "You mean she gave you the brush-off and you want some inside dope that's going to assure your seductive success?"

"Oh, come on, Maggie, it's not like that at all. She lives in this huge house outside of town, with walls around it like Fort Knox, and there are wild dogs running around in the grounds that could tear a man's leg off with a single bite."

"Maybe the Semples have a valuable art collection or something. Did you see the house itself?"

"I wasn't even allowed past the gates. She has this kind of chaperone, called Mathieu. He's a mute, and he looks like Jack Palance playing Dracula. When I faintly and meekly suggested that I might be allowed in I was given the rebuff of the century."

"You? Faint and meek?"

"I can be faint and meek when I want to. The trouble was, the whole place was off limits, no matter what kind of line I came out with. All I want to know is, what goes on there? I mean, Lorie Semple's a terrific-looking girl, and believe it or not I would like to get to know her better, but mainly I'm just curious."

"Do you think it could ever happen again?" Maggie asked wistfully.

"Do I think that *what* could ever happen again?"

"Us. You and me. The couple most likely to succeed. Isn't that what they said in the yearbook?"

"Maggie . . . I'm a young man. I have my whole life ahead of me."

"If you think that thirty-two's young, you ought to remember that it's only eight years away from forty."

He swallowed whiskey. "Okay, call me in eight years' time. But meanwhile, will you just do this one favor for me?"

"What do you want to know?"

"I want to know the Semple telephone number. I also want to know if Lorie ever goes out, and if she does, where she goes and how she spends her time. I would particularly like some photographs of the Semple estate, and some background on Jean Semple's death. Oh, and see if you can dig up anything on Mrs. Semple, Lorie's mother. It seems that she's quite a dragon in her own quiet way."

Maggie finished jotting down what he wanted. "How soon do you need this, as if I didn't know?"

"How about tomorrow?"

"Tomorrow's Sunday."

"That's all right—it won't interfere with your regular work. I'll be 'round at Walter's office most of the morning. Why don't you come by with the stuff, and I'll take you to lunch."

"That a promise?"

"God's honor. You think I'd tell you lies on the Sabbath?"

"No more than usual. By the way, what are you eating?"

"Nothing. What do you mean?"

"You sound like you're eating something," she said.

He touched his sensitive tongue. "Oh, that. No, I'm not eating anything. I just have this troublesome mouth ulcer, that's all."

"Okay, Gene. See you tomorrow. Don't forget, now. Lunch."

"Bye, bye, my darling Maggie."

He laid down the phone. He knew it was insensitive to ask Maggie to look up Lorie Semple's background, and he felt more than a little guilty about it, but she was the only person he knew that could do it thoroughly, discreetly, and fast. If he asked Mark Wellman to do it, or any of the other male members of his political staff, he knew that the story of the bitten tongue and the lost shoe would be buzzing around Washington in fifteen minutes flat. As it was, his name was probably already being romantically linked with Lorie's, and that was going to make his investigations less than easy.

He tried to decide if he wanted another drink. He was beginning to feel tired and his body was beginning to ache, and in the end he wearily undressed and took a long shower, standing under the gushing water and thinking about Lorie Semple. In his mind, he ran through the whole evening again, from the moment when he stepped up to her with his hand held out, to the disturbing feel of her breast through the thin material of her dress.

He soaped himself, and in soaping himself, he suddenly realized just how much Lorie Semple turned him on.

They went to a little brunch place not far from Walter Farlowe's office, sat behind the green glass of a bay window, and ordered steak and eggs. The place was a favorite with political staff who were working on Sundays, and it was already crowded when they arrived. An experienced observer could have divided the Republicans from the Democrats at a glance, and seen that while the donkeys tended to sit around the sweet trolley at the back of the room, the elephants gravitated to the windows.

Maggie was looking her usual fresh and wholesome self. She was a petite and pretty brunette, with a smatter of freckles across her uptilted nose and wide brown eyes. She always reminded Gene of the girls who used to greet homecoming doughboys on the covers of the *Saturday Evening Post*. Maybe that's why he hadn't married her years ago. They had been childhood sweethearts back in Jacksonville, and at the age of seventeen they had become lovers and stayed entangled until they were twenty-one.

Then Gene's political ambitions had called him, and Maggie had gone away to college, and somehow the most likely love affair faltered and dwindled, and they both went their own ways. Gene had fallen in love with a wealthy married woman almost twice his age and had been emotionally turned inside-out, while Maggie fell for a super-jock from Yale and had been through all the traumas of unwanted pregnancy and abortion.

They were back together again now because they were friends, and because the whole Democratic theme for the new administration had been Southern togetherness.

Gene tore bread, and chewed it in large pieces.

"Did you manage to get it?" he asked her.

She grinned. "You'll get fat, you know, eating as much bread as that!"

"Nobody could get fat on what I eat. Do you know what I had last night? One crab pastry and two Jack Daniels. I was so hungry in Walter's meeting this morning that my guts were rumbling."

Maggie picked her tapestry bag off the floor and probed inside it. She brought out her shorthand notebook, and opened it up.

"I got most of it," she said, "with the single exception of Lorie Semple's telephone number. For that, we have to wait until the phone company reference office opens on Monday morning."

Gene coughed. "I'm an important politician, and I have to wait till Monday morning? Did Jack Kennedy ever have to wait till Monday morning? Did LBJ?"

"Oh, I expect so," said Maggie. "The point was, I wanted to do this quietly and not cause a ruckus. I've already had a call from Senator Hasbaum's secretary this morning, asking how you made out with the gorgeous Ms. Semple, and if I were you I'd keep this particular romance out of the papers."

"Romance? Who said anything about romance? If you call a sprained ankle and a bitten tongue romance . . ."

Maggie blinked at him. "I thought you said it was an ulcer."

Gene shrugged, embarrassed. "Well, it's a similar kind of feeling. Ulcer, bite. Hard to tell the difference."

Maggie flipped over a few pages in her book. "The Semple house is quite interesting. It stands in forty acres of its own ground in Merriam. Most of the grounds are scrub and woods and I've been promised an aerial photograph. The house is a fifteen-bedroom ante-bellum mansion originally built by a Virginia tobacco grower. It was owned by various planters and politicians until it fell into disuse in 1911. It was empty until the Semples bought it in 1973, when Jean Semple was appointed to the staff of the French diplomatic staff in Washington, and they've lived there ever since."

Their steak and eggs arrived, and Gene lavished black pepper onto his plate while Maggie continued to read from her book.

"Jean Semple is—or was, rather—a very educated and wealthy man. He was born in 1919, in Sassenage, in Isere, of rich parents, and it looks like his family always expected him to make it in the diplomatic service. He went to Egypt in 1951 as a junior diplomat, and that's where he met his wife, Leila. There is hardly any information on her, except that her maiden name was Misab, and she spent most of her early life in the Soudan. Their only child, Lorie, was born eighteen years ago in Paris.

"Jean was always keen on wildlife. He gave quite a lot of money to various wildlife charities, particularly the national parks in Africa. But he was also a hunter, and it was while he was hunting that he was mauled by bears and killed. I have a Canadian coroner's report on its way."

Gene forked a piece of steak into his mouth, and then frowned.

"Is that all?" he asked her. "What about valuables? Did he collect anything? I mean—why is the house so fiercely guarded?"

"Nothing at all," said Maggie. "I talked to a couple of French diplomats who knew him, and they both said that he never collected anything much, and that all they knew about him was that he liked his privacy. Oh, and they also said that his wife was very beautiful, with what one of them called *une grande poitrine*."

"What's *une grande poitrine*?"

"Big knockers. I would have thought that even *your* French could have stretched to that."

"Stop being sarcastic and eat your steak."

They finished their meal, and afterward they walked together past the White House to Gene's office. It was a gray, humid day, in that indecisive period between September and October, when the Washington weather can never make up its mind. Up above them, unseen, a jet roared down toward Dulles Airport, throttling its way along the difficult flight path over the Potomac.

When they reached the silent, pillared portico of Gene's office, they held hands briefly. "Thanks for the lunch," Maggie said. "That's the best steak I've had in weeks."

"It's a pleasure. Maybe we should do it more often."

"Do what?" she asked, feigning innocence.

He looked at her for a moment, and then he leaned forward and kissed her forehead. "Whatever it is that good friends do."

"You will be careful, won't you?"

"Careful?"

She pulled her knitted jacket tighter around her. "It's what one of those French diplomats said. I didn't tell you before because I thought it sounded ridiculous. But it's been nagging me."

"What was it? 'Beware of the dogs?' "

"No, it was stranger than that. After he told me all about Mrs. Semple and Lorie, he asked if anyone was interested in them as far as marriage was concerned. I said no, I didn't think so. But he said if anyone is, warn them about the dance."

"The *dance*? What the hell does that mean?"

"I don't know. I told you it sounded ridiculous. But I just thought you ought to know. Just in case."

Gene took her arm, and laughed. His laugh echoed in the portico, and sounded strangled and peculiar.

"My beautiful Maggie," he said, "the last thing I am about to do is marry Lorie Semple, let alone her mother. The way she treated me last night, I don't suppose I'll even *see* her again, let alone get the opportunity to pop the question."

"I don't know," said Maggie. "I've always pictured you with hordes of kids and a station-wagon, and a suburban house in Grand Rapids."

"With Lorie Semple? You've got to be joking."

Maggie shrugged. "It's going to hit you one day. There was one time when I thought it would have to be me."

Gene stood there with his dark curly hair blown into tangles by the afternoon breeze. He had a square, Democratic-candidate kind of face, but like all Democrats it was capable of looking sensitive and sad as well as confident and vigorous.

"Maggie . . ." he said. But she shook her head and turned away from him.

"It doesn't matter," she told him gently. "Whatever you do, provided it's the best for you, it doesn't matter."

Then she walked off down the street and left him standing under the tall and dignified porch of his chosen profession.

About an hour later, he switched off his desk lamp and took off his heavy-rimmed spectacles. The report was almost finished, and he reckoned he could tidy it up without too much work in the morning. Although it was gloomy in the office, the sky was still pale and luminous outside, and he guessed there were three or four hours of good daylight left. He shuffled the papers on his desk and then stood up. Maybe he should take a drive out to the Semple place and look again for himself.

An erotic vision of Lorie Semple had been floating around in the back of his mind all day, even during the West Indian meeting. He only had to close his eyes for a fraction of a second, and he could see that silky, sensuous body, and that beautiful feline face. He said to himself, out loud, "That women has gotten under my skin," and he tapped a True out of a crumpled pack and lit it.

Why not do what he'd suggested, and call on her? There had to be a visitor's bell somewhere at the main gate, and maybe if he rang it and announced himself, instead of trying to sneak over the wall like a second-class yegg, he might get himself admitted to the house the respectable way. He just hoped that Lorie hadn't found his shoe.

He locked up his filing-cabinet, switched off all the office lights, and went out to get his car. It was nearly five by the time he drove out of the city center, and the clouds were growing heavier and darker. On the car radio, a preacher was calling for "an end to iniquity, O Lord, and an end to all human suffering." He added his own prayer for an end to losing expensive footwear in gates.

It took him half an hour to find the narrow uphill road that led up to the Semple place, and he drove past it twice before he recognized it. In the daylight, it somehow looked different, although he knew he had taken the right turn-off when he drove through the overhanging tunnel of trees, and emerged at the crest of the hill by the high spiked wall. He turned the sharp corner, and there was the wrought-iron gate. The shoe, as he had feared, was gone.

He climbed out of the car and walked up to the bars. Even during the day, the Semple grounds looked gloomy and overcast, and the leaves of the oaks rustled sadly in the wind. The drive stretched ahead of him, and disappeared around the corner, and he knew that he was going to have to discover what lay beyond it. He stepped back a few paces, looking right and left, and eventually saw it. A small brass bell, with the name *Semple* engraved around it in Gothic lettering.

He pushed it, twice. Then he paced up and down, his ankles teased by tumbling leaves, waiting for someone to answer.

It was almost ten minutes before he saw any sign of life. Then he heard the whine of an electric motor, and around the corner in the drive appeared a bright red golf cart with a red-and-white striped awning, driven by the stoney-faced Mathieu.

The golf cart took almost five minutes to arrive at the gates. Mathieu halted it a few yards away, and dismounted. Then he walked up to Gene, and examined him through the bars.

"I've come to call on Lorie," said Gene, in a louder and more uncertain voice than he'd hoped. "If she's in, I'd like to say hello."

Mathieu appeared to give this some thought. Then he began to wave his hands backward and forward as if to say "no."

Gene stood there stubbornly. "Will you please just tell her I'm here?"

Again, Mathieu waved his hands. *No, monsieur, I won't.*

"Well, how about Mrs. Semple. Can I see her?"

No—and a flapping gesture that obviously meant *go away.*

"Mathieu," said Gene insistently, "will you try to understand? I don't mean Lorie any harm. I'm not a Casanova. I just want to say hello and ask her out for dinner."

No. Go away.

"Look," said Gene. "Let's be sensible about this, huh?" He took out his wallet, and produced a ten-dollar bill, which he folded between his fingers and poked through the gates. "Will you just let me in?"

Mathieu stared at the bill with icy, relentless eyes. Then he looked back at Gene, and there was such intense contempt on his face that Gene withdrew the bill and tucked it hastily and untidily back in his wallet. At that particular moment, he was extremely glad that there was half a ton of iron gate in between him and this mute kravmaga freak.

"All right," Gene said. "If I can't persuade you, I can't persuade you. But will you just take a message? Will you tell Lorie to call me? Please?"

Mathieu looked at him coldly for a few more moments and then turned around and walked back to his golf cart. With a high-pitched whine, he trundled off again down the drive and disappeared from sight behind the trees. Gene leaned against the gates and sighed.

He was about to return to his car when he thought he saw something in the distance, almost hidden by the long grass. He screwed up his eyes, and for one fleeting second he saw Lorie, walking slowly among the trees with a big dog on a leash. She was wearing blue slacks and a billowing white blouse, her tawny hair brushed back and floating in the wind.

Gene yelled, "Lorie! Lorie!" But she was too far away and before he could shout again she was gone.

He went back and sat in his New Yorker, drumming his fingers on the steering wheel and wondering what to do next. He didn't fancy trying to break into the Semple estate in broad daylight. Nor did it help ringing the visitor's bell. All he could do now was to wait for the morning, when Maggie would hopefully have the telephone number. Then perhaps he could get past the impassive Mathieu and talk to Lorie herself, or at least her mother.

He drove back to the city, feeling disappointed, but increasingly determined. If ever he'd faced an up-and-up challenge, this was it, and no matter what it took, he was damned if he wasn't going to lick it.

Monday morning was bright, with a slight snap of winter in the air, and Gene wore his overcoat to work. He reached his office early, just before eight, but Maggie was even earlier. She was sitting at her desk with a plastic cup of coffee, smoking a cigarette and hanging on the phone.

Gene hung up his coat. "Who is it?" he mouthed. "Anyone I shouldn't talk to?"

Maggie put her hand over the receiver. "It's my secret Monday-morning lover. Keep your mouth shut, or he'll hear you."

Gene went to his desk and flipped quickly through his stack of mail. There was a whole pile of letters from the West Indies, and some irritating enquiries about subsidy policy in parts of Central America. Even if he got down to it straight away, this particular bundle was going to take him most of the morning to answer, and he still had to finish a report on West Indian internal affairs. He tapped a True out its pack and lit up.

Maggie was saying: "Uh-huh. Okay, I gotcha. Thanks, Marvin. I owe you one." Then she put the phone down and came across to Gene with a self-satisfied smile. She was wearing a neat rust-colored suit today, and not for the first time he realized just how pretty she really was.

"Well?" he asked, frowning over a six-page letter on sugar production. "You look like the cat who cornered the cream market."

"And why shouldn't I? You asked the impossible, o boss, and the impossible has been accomplished."

She tore a page from her shorthand pad and put it down in front of him. On it was written First Bank of Franco-Africa, 1214 K Street, and under that was a telephone number.

He picked it up. "What's this? Something to do with Lorie Semple?"

"Only her telephone number," said Maggie smugly. "And only the address of the bank where she works."

Gene raised an eyebrow. "She works? You mean she doesn't spend her whole life shut up in that house at Merriam?"

"Of course not. Why should she do that?"

"I don't know," said Gene. "The way that place is guarded, it seems like they lock themselves in there and never come out."

Maggie stubbed her cigarette out. "That's a typical chauvinist attitude. If they won't swoon at your feet and beg you to take them to bed, they must be living some kind of mysterious existence locked up in a weird old house. I mean, it's the only explanation."

"You didn't see the size of those goddamn guard dogs. They were this big."

"They were probably friendly St. Bernards coming to rescue you. If you hadn't panicked, they might even have given you a tot of brandy."

Gene checked his watch. If he took a cab, he might get up to the Franco-African Bank before it opened, which meant that he could catch Lorie in the street. "Listen, Maggie," he said. "I'm going out. I won't be long. If Walter calls, or if Mark starts sniffing around, just say that I'm out on an urgent diplomatic call. I'll be back in half an hour."

"Gene," said Maggie, warningly. "Don't let this business go to your head. If the lady really doesn't want to know you, don't go making a fool of yourself."

"Maggie," he said, shucking on his coat, "did I ever make a fool of myself?"

"Only once," she said tartly, and went back to her desk.

He stepped out into the street and hailed a cab. The driver was a silent black with a huge, pungent cigar, and by the time they reached K Street, Gene was glad to get out into the chilly October air. He paid the driver, tipped him, and then walked over to the wide stainless steel doors of the Franco-African Bank. A small delegation of Algerians was waiting there, too, shuffling their feet and talking to each other in thickly accented French. Gene couldn't catch everything they said, but he gathered that they'd been disappointed by the Jefferson Memorial. One of them said it reminded him of a sports pavilion.

A few minutes before the bank was due to open, two girls came walking down K Street and joined the waiting customers. They looked to Gene like tellers, and so he stepped across with a hesitant smile. "Ladies?" he said.

They turned and stared at him blankly. One of them

had upswept spectacles, and the other was chewing gum with such relentless energy that every muscle in her face was working away like a rubber mask.

"Excuse me," said Gene, "but do you ladies work here?"

"What's it to you?" said the one with the gum.

"Well," said Gene, feeling embarrassed, "it's just that a friend of mine works here, and I was wondering if you knew her. Her name's Lorie Semple."

"Lorie? Sure. She's in the foreign exchange department."

"Do you know if she's coming in to work today?" asked Gene.

"Never known her to miss a day," said the girl with the gum. "She's real fit, you know. Exercises a lot. Isometrics, all that."

"Are you her boyfriend?" asked the girl with upswept spectacles.

Gene shook his head. "Oh, no, nothing like that. Just a friend."

"She could do with a boyfriend," said the girl, knowingly.

"Why?" said Gene. "Do you think she's lonely?"

"Oh, I don't know. She's kind of wistful. You know what I mean by wistful? She talks about getting married a lot, and she's a cute looker but she never has any boyfriends. Maybe there's something in her personality, you know. Also, she's very tall. I don't think boys really go for girls that tall."

"My Sam says dating her would be like dating the New York Nets. You know?" said the girl with the gum.

Gene continued. "I know it seems kind of personal to ask you this, but do you like her?"

"Oh, sure," said the girl with the gum. "Lorie's a

sweet kid. Real sweet. You couldn't dislike her if you tried. But then she's pretty hard to get to know. I mean, I don't even know where she lives. How can you dislike someone if you don't know anything about them?"

As the girl was talking, Gene glimpsed a black Cadillac limousine drawing in to the curb. Instinctively, he guessed it was Lorie, and he bent his knees slightly so that he was hidden from sight behind the chattering group of Algerians.

"Is there something wrong with your knees?" asked the girl with the upswept spectacles.

Gene grinned. "No, no. Just doing my on-the-spot exercises. Hold still for a moment, would you?"

He heard the limousine stop, and then the back door opened, paused, and slammed. Footsteps came tapping across the sidewalk, and the limousine pulled away and joined the honking K Street traffic. He stood up to his full height, and there she was.

In her working clothes, she looked, if anything, more beautiful. She was wearing an immaculately tailored black suit with a high-shouldered jacket and a pencil skirt, and a black 1950s-style hat. Her golden-brown hair was severely pinned back, but that only emphasized the classic slant of her cheekbones and her bright green eyes. When she saw him she stopped at once, and held her black, snakeskin pocketbook close to her chest.

"Hello, Lorie," he said gently.

The two tellers looked from Gene to Lorie and back again, and the one with the gum gave the one with the upswept spectacles a quick nudge in the ribs.

Lorie said nothing at first, but stepped a few paces nearer, her eyes lowered, and her lips slightly parted.

"So you found me," she said, in that deep husky

voice of hers. "I suppose I knew that you would. Who told you?"

He shook his head, and smiled. "You're not that hard to find. My secretary's been working on it."

"Well," she said, "I suppose I should be flattered. An important man like you, taking so much trouble over someone as insignificant as me."

"Don't be ridiculous. I wanted to see you."

She looked up. Her green eyes widened. This girl is incredibly beautiful, he thought. She's like some kind of fantasy. How can a girl be this beautiful and so stand-offish at the same time? It simply doesn't make sense.

"After Saturday night, I didn't think you'd want to." Lorie said.

"Of course I did. The one animal that intrigues me is a girl that bites. I was 'round on Sunday, ringing at the bell, but I don't suppose Mathieu told you that."

"You came yesterday?"

"Sure I did. You think Saturday night's little misunderstanding would put me off?"

"I don't understand. I thought I made it clear that I didn't want to see you any more."

"About as clear as Mississippi mud. One minute you said you liked me, and the next minute you were treating my tongue like a Big Mac."

"I didn't mean to hurt you," she said. "Is it still sore?"

"Only when I lick."

She looked away, and a slice of early-morning sun illuminated her golden eyelashes and her unusual green eyes.

"I'm sorry it happened that way," she said quietly. "I wish it could have been different."

"It *could* have been different," he insisted. "In fact,

it could *still* be different now. I could take you to dinner tonight, and we could make up for Saturday night three times over."

She reached out and held his hand. Her fingers felt warm and slender, and her grip was firm.

"Gene," she said plainly, "I want to tell you that you're one of the most attractive men I've ever met. I like you more than you'll ever understand. That, and only that, is the reason why I won't go out with you."

He shook his head in bewilderment. "I thought *political* logic was screwy enough," he told her. "But I just don't grasp what you're saying. Are you frightened of getting too serious? Is that it? Are you worried about your own feelings?"

"No," she said softly. "It's nothing like that."

"Then what is it? For Christ's sake, Lorie, you have to tell me."

She simply said, "I can't."

He didn't know what else he could do to convince her. They stood side by side on the sunlit sidewalk until the doors of the Franco-African Bank were unlocked from the inside and opened, and then she touched his arm just once and walked in.

"Lorie," he said as she went.

She paused, but didn't look back.

He knew what he wanted to tell her, but he didn't have the words to explain what he felt, so he just turned away and walked off down K Street, his hands jammed in his coat pockets and his head bent. The girl with the upswept glasses tittered as he went off, until the girl with the gum said "Ssshhh," and hurried her into the bank.

He didn't really surprise himself when he finally came to the conclusion that he was going to have to sneak over the wall of the Semple estate and check the place out. It was the kind of blunt, straightforward thinking that had won him his job with the State Department, and particular favor with the Kennedy camp. His answer to every sensitive and puzzling diplomatic dilemma was to "get straight in there and find out what the hell's going on."

He was an uncomplicated thinker, but he was also a methodical man with a talent for detail, and he reckoned he could execute a one-man commando raid on the Semple estate with such precision that he could get in and out of the grounds without anyone ever knowing he was there. All he wanted to do was look over the house and the ground and hopefully gather one or two clues about Lorie Semple's stubborn insistence that any kind of romance between them was out of the question.

Ever since Monday morning, Lorie had become an increasingly alluring obsession. He knew how adolescent his infatuation was, but there was nothing he could do to get her out of his mind. He doodled her name on his blotting pad, and even tried to sketch pictures of her face. And what made it worse was the way that her words kept coursing through his mind. *I want to tell you that you're one of the most attractive men I've ever met. I like you more than you'll ever understand.*

"You," said Maggie, setting a styrofoam cup of coffee down on his desk, "have got it bad."

"Got what bad?" he said.

"The dreaded Lorie Semples. A disease known to modern medical science as rampant puppy love. That's what."

He sipped his coffee and scalded his lip.

"I deny it categorically," he told her. "And apart

from that, how can anyone of thirty-two suffer from puppy love?"

"Don't ask me," she said with a shrug. "Just ask the person who wrote Lorie Semple twenty-four times on your best blotting paper."

"You expect me to use that cheap purple stuff, for *her*?"

Maggie sat down and leaned confidingly on his desk. "Come on, Gene," she said quietly, "why don't you admit it? I haven't seen you like this for years."

He sipped some more coffee.

"All right, I admit it. She's stuck in my mind and I can't get her out. It's the ridiculous way that she says she likes me, and at the same time says we can never go out together. It's driving me crazy, if you must know."

"What are you going to do about it?" she asked.

He sat there for a while, drinking his coffee in quick, burning mouthfuls, trying to make up his mind whether he ought to tell her or not. In the end, he decided in favor. Maggie's thinking was always level and logical, and always sympathetic, too.

"I'm working out a plan," he said slowly, "I want to break into the Semple estate."

Maggie sat back. "You're working out a plan to do *what*?"

"Maggie," he said, "I've *got* to know. Breaking in there, finding out for myself, that's the only way. I've got to see what it is that makes her so reluctant. I mean, maybe it's her mother. Maybe the old girl's crippled, and Lorie doesn't want to get herself involved with anyone who's going to take her away from nursing her."

"Gene, you're out of your mind. Supposing you get caught?"

He shook his head. "Not a hope. I've worked it out that I can get in there, snoop around a little, and get out again with no problems."

"There are dogs. Dogs as big as this. You said so yourself."

"Even dogs as big as that get thrown off by gas. I'm going to take a few of those sprays that mail carriers use. It's suppose to stun them for long enough to take a letter up someone's drive, and that will be long enough for me."

"What about the chauffeur, Mathieu?"

"He won't even know I'm there. In case he does find out, I'm taking a .38. I won't use it, of course, but if he's such a kravmaga expert, I'd prefer to have something to wave around in self-defense."

Maggie sat there biting her lip for a long time. "Can I persuade you not to do it?" she asked after a while.

"I don't think so. I've made up my mind."

"Even though it might ruin your career?"

He reached for a cigarette. "It won't do that, even if I'm caught red-handed. All I have to say is that I was paying her a visit, and that the .Semples mistakenly took me for a prowler. Christ, Maggie, I'm not going to *burglarize* the place. I'm only going to take a quick look around the grounds and maybe a fast check through the windows."

"You're paying a visit? At night? With a loaded gun?"

"Maggie, you're just making things sound awkward. All I'm going to do is hop over the wall. The place is enormous, they'll never see me."

She thought for a moment longer, and then she stood up.

"You really fell head over heels this time, didn't you?"

He looked up. "And what's wrong with that? It's about time there was more committed passion in life, anyway."

"You're probably right," Maggie said. "But it depends where it's directed, don't you think?"

It was a few minutes after eleven Thursday night when he arrived outside the Semple mansion. He was driving a rented, dark-blue Matador, and he was dressed in a black, polo-neck sweater, black corduroy pants, and a charcoal-gray cap pulled down over his eyes. He carried a small canvas bag with Mace gas and anti-dog sprays, a coil of rope around his shoulder, and a long-barreled .38 revolver tucked into his belt. He switched off the car's engine and sat there for four or five minutes, listening to the soft rustle of the night.

This time, he had driven past the main gates and followed the road that led around the high brick wall to a point that, he hoped, was nearer the house itself. He had parked the car in the shadow of the overhanging trees on the opposite side of the road, and he left the keys in the ignition in case he needed to make a quick getaway.

It was a chilly night, and his breath steamed as he climbed out of the car and gently clicked the door shut behind him. Low clouds were still obscuring the moon, and he had to blink a few times to accustom his eyes to the darkness. He listened again, holding his breath, but the Semple estate was silent.

Quickly, he padded across the narrow road, trod softly through the banked-up leaves against the wall, and paused. Still no sound from the Semple place. He unwound a knotted nylon rope from his waist, and stepped back so that he could judge the height of the old, moss-crusted bricks. There was an aluminum rod tied to the end of the rope, and he hoped to toss this over the wall and tug it back until it was firmly wedged between the metal spikes.

It took four tries. The first time, he threw too short, and the next two shots went over but the rod refused to catch. At last he had the rope firmly in position, and he started to climb up it, gasping and sniffing and praying that the old rusted spikes were strong enough to take his weight.

In three minutes he had scrambled up to the top. He sat astride the wall, winding the rope and catching his breath. Through the trees he could see twinkling lights from the Semple mansion, but there was no sound at all, and no sign of the prowling guard dogs. A freight train hooted mournfully in the distance and up above the clouds a jet scratched its way across the night sky.

When the rope was wound in, he positioned the aluminum rod on the other side of the spikes, and let the rope down on the Semple side of the wall. Then he gently slithered off the top, swinging down to the ground with his feet scraping on the brick. Once he reached the bottom he paused again, his ears pricked up, hiding as deeply as he could in the dark shadow of the wall and the trees.

He checked his watch. It was a quarter after eleven. He straightened the revolver in his belt, and began to stalk carefully through the long grass, stopping every few moments to listen. He just hoped that if he needed to climb back up his rope in a hurry, he could remember where it was.

It took him ten minutes to make his way through the scrubby copse that led towards the house. There was still no sign of the dogs, and he wondered if they were asleep. Maybe if he was quiet enough he wouldn't wake them. He pushed his way through a tangled screen of bushes, and found himself on the very edge of the copse, with a wide stretch of lawn between him and the Semple mansion.

The house itself was much larger than he had anticipated. It was brooding and morose, with ranks of chimneys and twisting rivers of leafless creeper down every wall. There was a verandah around the southwest corner, which was the part of the house nearest to him, but all the windows around it seemed to be empty and dark. Further back, on the south side, there was a stately columned porch, but like everything else it was tangled with creeper and had a desolate, decayed air about it. The only window that seemed to be lit was an upstairs bay on the western side, and the drapes were drawn so tight that it was impossible to see inside.

Gene skirted along the southern side of the house, almost as far as the gravel drive that came from the main gateway. Every now and then he stopped to listen for dogs, but the whole estate was buried deep in darkness and silence. At one time, he thought he heard a faint crackling of leaves and twigs, but when he paused to catch the sound more distinctly, he realized it was probably just a bird in the upper branches of the oaks.

None of the windows on the south side were lit, so he went back to the edge of the copse and surveyed the west side again. There was a strong creeper which grew from the end of the verandah and twisted its way quite close to the lighted window. Gene reckoned that if he climbed up there, he could probably get his footing on the narrow gutter that extended under the window from the verandah roof and get a glimpse through a small crack in the drapes. The thought that he might see Lorie made his heart pound.

Ducking low, he ran across the open lawn until he

reached the verandah. He waited awhile and then went up the verandah's four wooden steps, taking care not to tread on the empty frames of abandoned deckchairs and the pieces of a garden swing. He walked softly along the whole length of the verandah, concealed in shadow, until he reached the end of it, where the trunk of the creeper grew.

Again, he listened. He thought he could hear faint voices and the sound of music, but that was all. The low, gray clouds still blotted out the moon, although a faint luminescence illuminated the lawns and distinguished the copse as a dark sea that rustled and washed around it.

Gene perched himself up on the verandah railing, and reached around to test the strength of the creeper. Years ago, someone had nailed it pretty firmly to the wall, and he guessed it would probably take his weight. He hung on to it with one hand, and then swung himself around and held on to it with both. There was a lurching noise as some of the dry branches gave way, but the main branch seemed to hold.

Breathing with tense, suppressed gasps, he reached up for higher branches and began to scale the creeper like a ladder. At a height of about ten or twelve feet, almost level with the verandah roof, he paused once more and listened for sound of the dogs. He heard a low, erratic, rumbling noise, but he guessed it was a distant airplane turning toward Dulles.

At last he was able to reach out his left foot and cautiously test the guttering. Further along it was rusted through, but from the verandah roof to the bay window it looked as if it was reasonably intact. He pressed on it with more weight, and then decided to try his luck and stand on it with both feet with his full 192 pounds. The lighted window was now only two or three feet away, and he could hear voices more distinctly and the creak of floorboards as someone walked around in the room.

It happened at the very instant he was stepping on to the guttering. There was a loud, hair-raising snarl, and something immensely powerful and heavy leaped up at him from the ground and tore him bodily down from the creeper. His fingers and face were lacerated as the beast's weight dragged him straight through branches and leaves and brought him to the grass with a back-bruising thump. Then the thing rolled on top of him, slavering and snarling and tearing at him with vicious claws. Gene smelled a rank animal odor that was anything but dog, and he screamed in desperation as his sweater was ripped away from his arms, and guzzling jaws bit into his shoulder muscle to tug the flesh away from his collar bone.

Three

Gene opened his eyes. It was obviously morning. He was lying in a narrow brass bed in a small upstairs room with floral wallpaper. A watery sunlight was falling across the room and touching the top of a walnut chiffonier, on which, from where he lay, he could see a wooden camel with a decorated saddle, and a black-and-white photograph in a silver frame of a woman who could have been Lorie's grandmother.

His shoulder was stiff and throbbed with suppressed pain. When he turned his head, he saw that it was tightly bandaged. There were dark brown marks on the bandage that probably were dried blood. He coughed and realized that his ribs were bruised, too.

For an hour or so he drifted into sleep and out again. It occurred to him during one of his waking moments that he was probably under sedation. He had strange nightmares about pale and ferocious beasts with claws, and he woke up one time shouting.

Around mid-morning, the door of his room opened. He moved his head, and through blurry eyes he saw a tall woman standing there. He thought for one moment it was Lorie, but then he saw that this woman was older, and more dignified. She was wearing a dove-gray dress, and her silver hair was elaborately coiffed and covered with a pearl-studded hairnet. She had a magnificent figure for a woman in her midfifties, with big heavy breasts and a slender waist. He suddenly remembered Maggie's words about *une grande poitrine*. This, evidently, was Lorie's mother.

"Mr. Keiller," she said, in a soft French accent. "Are you awake now, Mr. Keiller?"

He nodded. "I feel lousy. My throat's dry."

She sat on the edge of his bed and lifted a blue glass of mineral water. With firm hands, she raised his head for him, and he drank. Afterwards, she patted his lips with a tissue.

"Is that better?" she asked.

"Thank you, yes."

Mrs. Semple sat and looked at him with quite unabashed interest.

"You were very lucky, you know," she said, after a moment.

"Lucky? I feel like I'm half-dead."

"Half-dead is better than completely dead, Mr. Keiller. You were lucky you were so close to the house. If you had been further away, we might not have reached you in time."

"Do you *train* your dogs to do that?"

She put her head on one side and frowned a little, as if she couldn't quite understand what he was saying.

"To kill," he prompted. "To tear people apart."

She nodded vaguely. "Yes," she said. "I suppose we do."

"You *suppose*? I practically died out there!"

Mrs. Semple didn't look particularly concerned. "You shouldn't really have been out there in the first place, should you, Mr. Keiller? We did try to warn you!"

"Yes," he said. "I guess you're right. But all the same, those dogs are something else. Is my arm all right?"

"You'll survive. I bandaged it myself. I used to do . . . nursing of a kind . . . out in Egypt."

Gene tried to sit up, "All the same," he said. "I think I'd better get to a hospital. I'm going to need tetanus and rabies jabs."

Mrs. Semple pressed him gently back against the bed with the palm her hand. "You've already had them, Mr. Keiller. It was the first thing I did. There really is no need to do anything but rest for a while."

"Do you have a phone I could use?"

"You want to call your office?"

"Well, naturally. I have a couple of big meetings today, and I'm going to have to cry off."

Mrs. Semple smiled. "Don't worry. We've already phoned your secretary and told her you're sick. Someone called Mark is going to stand in for you."

Gene lay back and looked at Mrs. Semple curiously. "You're very considerate," he said, although it was more of a question than a compliment.

"You're my *guest*," said Mrs. Semple. "Our people are always considerate to guests. Anyway, Lorie has been talking about you a lot, and I've been most anxious to make your acquaintance. You're not at all like she said you were."

"Oh? Am I better, or worse?"

Mrs. Semple smiled, almost dreamily. "Oh, you're better, Mr. Keiller—much, much better! The way Lorie spoke about you, anyone would have thought you were a mixture of Quasimodo and Frankenstein's monster. But you're not, are you? You're young, and you're rather good-looking, and you work for the State Department, too."

Gene rubbed his eyes. "I must say, Mrs. Semple, I haven't been able to figure Lorie out."

"You like her though, don't you? You find her attractive?"

"Well, sure. That's mostly the reason I'm here."

"I thought you did. You . . . well, you talked a great deal under sedation. You mentioned Lorie several times."

"I hope I didn't say anything too basic."

Mrs. Semple laughed. "Don't worry about that, Mr. Keiller. I'm a very sophisticated woman, and I know how sexually appealing my daughter is. You did say . . . one or two things."

Gene coughed. His ribs felt as if they'd been leaned on by elephants and even his spine was bruised.

"Well," he said, "if I was too crude or anything, I'm sorry. I can't hide the fact that I find Lorie very attractive."

"Why should you? You're obviously an impulsive sort of a man."

He winced as he tried to sit up. "In this case, a little *too* impulsive, I'm afraid."

Mrs. Semple leaned forward and plumped up his pillow for him. For one moment her warm body brushed against him, and he caught the same distinctive scent that he had smelled on Lorie.

"I think we can happily forget about last night, Mr. Keiller," she said gently. "After all, I don't think either of us would care for a fuss, and newspaper gossip, would we?"

Gene looked at her carefully. She was trying to be nonchalant, but he sensed an unusual tension about her as she waited for his answer. Her fingers drummed nervously on the patchwork counterpane, and she kept giving him little spasmodic smiles.

"I know this is kind of impertinent," he said slowly,

"but can I ask you what you've got here that requires guarding so fiercely?"

Mrs. Semple touched her forehead with her finger-tips as if she felt a slight headache coming on. "We have nothing of value, Mr. Keiller, except our privacy. Having this place to ourselves means a great deal to us."

"I guess you're entitled to it," said Gene, "and you mustn't think that I'm trying to teach you to suck eggs. But don't you think Lorie should get out more? She seems pretty lonely."

"My dear Mr. Keiller. I'm always trying to persuade her."

Gene coughed. "That wasn't the impression I got from her. She really implied that it was you who was holding her back."

Mrs. Semple nodded. "You're not the first," she said, in a weary voice.

"She told me she'd never dated anyone."

"That's quite right, Mr. Keiller, she never has. But it certainly wasn't for lack of encouragement on my part, and it certainly wasn't for lack of enthusiasm on the part of the poor fellows who tried to take her out. She's nineteen, you know, and I do feel it's time she went out into the world and got herself some experience with men."

"Mrs. Semple, if I were to ask Lorie out, would you encourage that, too?"

"Of course!" laughed Mrs. Semple in a rather forced tone. "I don't see how anyone could be more eligible! You're precisely the type of man I've always had my eye on."

"Well, I'm very flattered, Mrs. Semple, but I'm not sure I've got marriage in mind. I'm afraid my career is pretty important to me."

Mrs. Semple stood up and walked over to the window. The fall sunlight somehow made her look even taller than she had seemed before, and Gene was surprised to see that the roots of her hair were as tawny as Lorie's. The silver-gray look must have been hair dye. She turned back and stared at him with those glittering and hypnotic green eyes that characterized the female side of the Semple family, and she said softly: "If you like, I will speak to Lorie, and see if I can't persuade her to change her mind."

"I get the feeling there's some kind of condition placed on that."

"Condition?" said Mrs. Semple, lifting one eyebrow. She pronounced the word the French way—*condission*. She didn't look surprised at what he had said.

Gene shifted himself into a more comfortable position. "Supposing I forget about the dog last night? Is that the kind of deal you had in mind?"

Mrs. Semple smiled a long, lazy smile. "You don't work for the State Department for nothing, do you? You have read my thoughts."

"In that case," said Gene, "it's a deal."

When the pain in his shoulder came back, Mrs. Semple gave him another shot of sedative, and he slept in dreaming jigsaw-pieces from lunch until early evening, muttering and mumbling and tossing in his sleep. Sometimes he thought he saw Mrs. Semple standing in his room, and at other times he thought he was being watched by a strange animal that regarded him with cold and emotionless eyes.

The strangest dream he had was that someone was arguing in another room—a long and loud and persistent argument that he couldn't quite hear or understand. He caught the words "eligible" and "perfect" over and over again, and then the words "ritual" and "frightened" seemed to follow. He couldn't be sure if it was the same dream or not, but after that he heard animals snarling and tussling, and the dream turned into a nightmare about heavy beasts tearing him down from the wall and sinking their teeth into his arm.

He woke up and there was something cool on his forehead. He opened his eyes and Lorie was sitting on the chair beside his bed, leaning over and holding a cold compress against his brow. He realized he was sweating and trembling, and his mouth was dry as ash.

"Lorie," he croaked.

"I'm here, Gene," she said quietly. "Don't worry. You've just had a nightmare, that's all. It's the sedative."

He tried to turn his head. "What time is it?" he asked her.

"Half after seven. You've been asleep since one."

"I think . . ." he said, stretching his muscles as much as he could, ". . . I think I feel better."

"Mother says you should be able to get up tomorrow. She phoned your office again and told them. Someone called Maggie sends you her love."

Gene nodded. "That's my secretary. She's a nice girl."

There was an awkward silence between them. Lorie lifted the compress away, took it over to the washbasin, and wrung it out. Then she ran the cold faucet, testing the water with the tip of her finger. Gene watched her without saying a word. She looked twice as beautiful as she had when he had first seen her, and he felt pleased and amazed that someone could attract him more and more each day as she did. She was wearing a plum-colored silk blouse with embroidered cuffs, and superbly tailored beige slacks. Her wrists were jangling with gold bracelets, and around her neck, deep between her breasts, she wore a golden pendant.

"Lorie," said Gene, as gently as he could.

She didn't turn around, but he could see she was watching him in the circular mirror above the basin. The pupils of her eyes were dilated and dark.

"You're not . . . frightened of anything, are you?" he asked her.

She turned off the faucet. "Why should I be?"

"I don't know. That's what I'm asking you. It's just that you give me that impression."

"There's nothing to be frightened of," she said, coming back to his bedside with the fresh compress. "We are not the kind of people who feel afraid."

"You seem to be afraid of intruders."

She stroked his hair back before laying the compress on his forehead. Her touch was very soft. Her curved lips were slightly open, and he saw her lick them with the tip of her tongue in a way that was innocent but also indescribably sensual.

"It depends who the intruders are," she said. "Some intruders we welcome."

"How about me? Am I welcome?"

She smiled slightly. "Of course you are. I told you before that I think you're attractive."

"You also told me to go away."

She lowered her eyes. "Yes," she said, "I did."

Gene took the compress away from his forehead. Now that the effects of the sedative had completely worn off, he was fresher and brighter. His shoulder was healing—he could feel the sinews tightening and the skin growing scabs. There was still a dull muscular ache from bruises and bumps, but he could tolerate that. He was beginning to feel less like a helpless invalid and more like a bedridden politician.

"Lorie," he said, "can I use your telephone?"

She looked at him warily. "What for?"

"I need to call my office. There were a couple of big meetings today and I want to find out what happened."

"Mother said——"

"Lorie, I have to check up. It's my job. I can't just sit back here and let the United States drift rudderless and leaderless into World War Three."

Lorie seemed uncertain. "I don't know," she said. "Mother said that she'd rather you didn't call anyone."

He frowned. "What did she mean by that?"

"I'm not sure. I think she was worried you might call an attorney. You know, about your bites. She's very anxious that you don't tell anyone what happened."

"I've already promised that I wouldn't do that," Gene said cautiously.

Lorie blushed a little. "I know."

"She told you?"

"Yes. We had a row about it. She made me promise to go out with you in return."

Gene gave a humorless laugh. "Listen, I'm not going to force you. If you don't want to go out with me, if you really don't want to, then the last thing I'm going to do is blackmail you into doing it. I only want to take you out if you genuinely want to go."

She glanced at him, almost shyly.

"Well, do you?" he asked her. "If you don't, then the best thing we can do is retire gracefully and leave it at that."

She traced a pattern on the counterpane with her finger. "I was thinking of you," she said, in a soft and serious voice.

"I don't understand."

She reached out and held his hand. Her eyes were

anxious and intent, as if she was trying to tell him something without actually speaking it out loud—trying to communicate some warning that it was impossible to put into words.

"My mother is a believer in tradition, Gene." She said. "She likes things done in the way they always were. Some of her beliefs, and some of the things she does . . . well, you may not be able to accept them for what they really are."

He squeezed her hand. "I'm still as lost as ever. What kind of tradition? What do you mean?"

She shook her head. "I can't tell you. You can only find out for yourself. I hope you never have to."

He looked at her questionably for a while, and when he saw she wasn't going to say anything more, he let out a small sigh of resignation and settled back on his pillow.

"Lorie," he said. "I don't mind telling you that you are the most baffling person I ever met. Maybe I should write you up for the Reader's Digest."

She gave a sad little grin. "You mustn't think that I don't like you, Gene. And you mustn't think that I'm not flattered—*complimented*—because you tried to get into the house and find me. It was very romantic, and I'm only sorry you got hurt."

"Do I take that to mean that you *do* want to go out with me? Or is it another polite way of saying *arrivederci?*"

She looked at him in silence for a while, and he thought he saw her eyes moisten with tears. Then she leaned forward, her lips carefully closed, and kissed him.

"I want, very much, to go out with you," she whispered. "That's why my promise to mother wasn't difficult to make. But before we ever do, just swear me one thing."

"You and your mother are as full of qualifying clauses as a Senate bill."

"I mean it, Gene. Please."

He shrugged stiffly. "Tell me what it is, and I'll swear."

"You must absolutely swear that you will never ask me to marry you."

He stared at her in disbelief. He found her fascinating, and arousing, and he'd even admit that he'd made something of a fool of himself over her. But as for *marriage* . . .

"Lorie, honey," he told her, "if there's one thing that you can be sure that I'm not, it's a marrying kind of man. I have a good job, an entertaining lifestyle, lots of friends, and quite a lot of money. The last thing on my mind right at this moment in time is wedlock."

"And you'll swear?"

"Sure I'll swear!"

He raised his right hand, and in a deep and resonant tone said: 'I, Gene Keiller, being of sound mind and only slightly damaged body, do solemnly swear that I will never ask you, Lorie Semple, to be my wedded wife."

He was going to continue, but then he saw that her face was utterly grave. She was fingering her pendant and frowning at him as if he was swearing the oath of allegiance to the flag.

"Lorie," he said, "I'm not trying to make fun of this, but you have to admit it's a pretty wacky kind of promise."

She nodded. "I know what it must seem like. But, please, Gene, don't ever break your promise. It's the only protection you have."

"Huh?"

She leaned forward again, and lifted her golden pendant so that he could see it close up. He squinted at it, and saw that it was a small pyramid. He reached his hand up to touch it, but she pulled it away.

"Is that a clue?" he asked her.

She shook her head. "It's just to show you. The influence of the pyramid is very strange and powerful. It's just to show you what you have to protect yourself against."

"Lorie, I——"

"All you have to do is remember that I showed it to you. Please. That's all I ask."

He gazed at her classic, high-cheekboned face in the dying light of the day, and he felt as mystified as he had the first time he had tried to kiss her. But she was so serious, and so intense. "All right," he said, "I'll remember, if that's what you want."

Later that week Gene met Lorie at the front gates of the house. It was a crisp, dry day, and the brown, curled-up leaves sounded like crunching ginger-snaps under their feet. A little way down the drive, Mathieu was standing stolidly beside his red-and-white striped golf cart, his stony expression concealed behind reflecting sunglasses, so that he looked as though he had two pieces of clear blue sky instead of eyes.

Lorie was wearing a safari jacket and boots, and her hair was tucked up into a wide-brimmed bush hat. She had made her eyes so that they appeared even more luminous and enormous than ever.

Gene opened the door of his car for her, and she climbed in. Then he walked around to the driving-seat, waving to Mathieu on the way.

"Doesn't he like me, or something?" asked Gene, as he sat down behind the wheel.

"Mathieu? I don't think he likes or dislikes people in the normal sort of way. He just does his job."

"Well, his job obviously doesn't include waving to your weekend date."

Lorie laughed. "I can't imagine Mathieu waving at anyone, let alone you."

They drove down the winding road, through the tunnel of overhanging trees, and out onto the main highway. Gene turned the car away from Washington and out toward Frederick. Walter Farlowe had invited them out to his vacation home for drinks and a barbecue, along with some of the leading professional people who had assisted the Democratic cause with finance and moral support during the crucial stages of the election.

Gene's shoulder was still bound up in crêpe bandage, but his bite wound had almost completely healed and the bruises on his ribs had gradually faded. When Maggie had seen him on Monday, she had tried to persuade him to visit the doctor, but he remembered his promise to Mrs. Semple, and insisted he was fit.

"After all," he had told her, "cavemen got bitten by wild beasts, and they didn't have a friendly neighborhood MD to visit."

"Cavemen used to die a lot," Maggie had said sharply, and walked out of the office.

This was Gene's first date with Lorie. He had called her on Wednesday evening and asked her to come, and even though she had seemed hesitant at first, she was happy and excited now, and he couldn't resist glancing across the car and reveling in the sheer sexual beauty that she radiated. Whatever hang-ups she had about marriage and her mother, that wasn't going to stop them from having a great time at Walter's party, and then maybe some more intimate amusements to follow. She was a girl in a million, and if he hadn't been trying to play things a little cooler since his ill-fated raid on the Semple estate, he would have told her so.

They drove through sunlight, shadow, and whirling leaves. Walter's weekend place was right out in the country, and at this time of the year it was a refreshing and exhilarating drive.

"You know something?" said Lorie. "I'm so nervous!"

"What are you nervous about?"

"Us! You and me. I'm so, excited, I don't want any of this to end."

He grinned. "Maybe it doesn't have to."

But Lorie shook her head. "One day, it will have to. Whatever happens, however things go."

Gene stuck a cigarette in his mouth and pushed in the car's cigar lighter. "You shouldn't be such a pessimist," he told her. "Try living in the present for a change, instead of the future."

She looked at him. The radio was playing "Where Have All The Flowers Gone?" "We have to be warned about the future, Gene, or perhaps we won't get out of the present alive."

He lit his cigarette. "You sound like your mother."

"Yes," she said. "I'm my mother's child."

It took them an hour to reach Walter Farlowe's house. It was a split-level white-painted vacation home that had been designed for him by Edward Ocean, the young and irretrievably tacky architect. There was a pool, which was now scattered with floating leaves, and a wide patio that overlooked a deep valley of misty treetops and blue haze. Most of the guests were already there, and the sloping driveway was crowded with red Mercedes and silver Sevilles. A brick barbecue was sending up smoke signals that told of charred chops and curled-up steaks, and Walter Farlowe himself, in a chef's hat and yellow suspenders, was sweating and grinning and trying to serve everything out on soggy paper plates.

Gene parked his New Yorker, and they walked down the open-plan steps at the side of the house to the patio. With a feeling of great satisfaction, he saw heads turn and heard one or two low, appreciative whistles, which meant that Lorie in her safari suit was creating just the stir he'd hoped for.

They walked across the patio, and as they approached the barbecue, Walter Farlowe came out and greeted them.

"Gene! Glad you could make it! Sorry I can't shake hands—too greasy."

"This is Lorie," said Gene. "A new, but very dear, friend of mine."

Walter tipped his chef's hat. "I'm pleased to know you, Lorie. How do you like your steak?"

Lorie glanced at Gene, and then back at Walter.

"Well," she said huskily, "I like it pretty underdone."

Walter grinned. "How underdone is 'pretty underdone?' "

Lorie licked her lips. "A couple of seconds on each side."

"A couple of *seconds*?" laughed Walter. "Now that's practically raw!"

"Yes," said Lorie. "That's the way I like it."

They were finishing off their orders for food to Walter when a curly-haired girl in a silky yellow-and-green trouser suit came up and linked her arm through Gene's.

"Gene Keiller—of all people!"

"Hallo, Effie. How's the advertising business?"

"Terrific. Is this your new friend?"

"It certainly is. Lorie, this is Effie, an old buddy of mine from way back in Florida. Effie, this is Lorie Semple."

The two women smiled at each other with mutual suspicion.

"Gene, you *must* meet Peter Graves," said Effie. "He's my latest shrink, and he's absolutely and completely the *sanest* man in the whole world. He's right over here! Lorie, why don't you come with me and meet some of the ladies. Nancy Bakowsky is here, would you believe? You know, the lady from *Woman's Home Journal*?"

Lorie gave Gene a quick wink over her shoulder as Effie whisked her away to talk to the ladies. It was a conversational convention at thrashes like this that the men stuck with the men and the women stuck with the women, and any man who tried to horn in on the ladies' circle was considered a wolf, while any lady who hung around the men's circle was regarded as a potential whore. For that reason, the men rubbed elbows and swapped medium-dirty stag stories, while the women crowded together and talked about feminism and who was dallying with whom.

Gene, carrying a fresh vodkatini, found Peter Graves sitting by the edge of the pool alone. He was a young bald man with a thoughtful face and rimless spectacles. He dressed in the kind of Aertex sweatshirt and navy-blue jersey-knit pants that made you think he might be an athlete, or at least a devotee of jogging. You could have mistaken him for a hairless Dustin Hoffmann.

"Hi," said Gene. "Mind if I join you? Effie's been singing your praises, and I wouldn't like to miss the sanest man in the world."

Peter looked a little bewildered. "Is that what she said? That *proves* she needs treatment."

Gene sat down on a plastic sun-chair and took a sip of his drink.

"What kind of analysis are you into?" he asked. "These days it's all TA and do-it-yourself, as far as I can see."

Peter nodded. "Well, I'm pretty transactional, but I'm trying to relate it to the patterns of real social encounters, if you see what I mean."

"Not entirely."

Peter tugged at his nose thoughtfully. "Let me put it this way. I'm trying to introduce greater reality into TA, because in my opinion it's been failing to face up to what life is all about."

"Oh," said Gene. He reached in his pocket for his cigarettes, and lit one up. The smoke drifted across the pool. "Tell me, do you believe that people can get obsessive about not doing things they really want to do?"

"Like what?" asked Peter.

"Like my girlfriend there, Lorie. You see her—the one in the safari suit? She said she liked me from the moment she first met me, yet she's been giving me warnings the whole time about how I mustn't get serious, and she even made me swear not to marry her."

"That's not unusual. She's probably anxious about the possibility of being tied down."

Gene shook his head. "It's more than that. She keeps trying to give me the impression that there's something spooky going on in her life. She won't tell me exactly what it is, and I can't even guess what she's trying to get at. But she's always giving me forbidding threats about the dire consequences of forming any kind of relationship with her."

Peter sniffed. "Do you want me to talk to her?"

"You mean, analyze her?"

"No, just talk. It sounds like an interesting syndrome. Why don't you let me go over and chat for a few minutes? I can't say I'd hate it. She's a beautiful girl."

Gene looked across the pool to where Lorie was being introduced to Nancy Bakowsky. "Okay," he said, noncommittally. "If you don't mind being eaten alive by half the Democratic ladies in town."

Gene waited while Peter Graves padded over to the ladies' circle on grubby running shoes and spoke for a while in Lorie's ear. There seemed to be some very intense discussion going on between them, but Gene was distracted by Walter Farlowe, who brought him a plateful of steak and salad, and a plastic knife and fork to eat it with. He broke the fork on the first attempt, and spent the next ten minutes searching for a new one.

When he got back to the pool, Peter Graves was waiting for him, sipping a 7-Up and looking thoughtful. "Well?" Gene said.

Peter gave an uncertain smile.

"Did you talk? Did you get any inkling?"

Peter looked unhappy. "Well, in a manner of speaking, yes. But I'm not too sure if I discovered too much."

Gene chewed a mouthful of burned steak. "Are you trying to tell me that you couldn't figure her out?"

"Well, no," said Peter hesitantly. "But the truth is, she seems to believe that she's locked into some kind of predestined fate. You know? And she's worried that if you get involved with her, you're going to get yourself involved in that predestined fate too."

"What do you mean, predestined fate?"

"Exactly that," explained Peter. "She thinks that, for one reason or another, her life has to follow a particular traditional pattern. She told me that. And when I asked her about you, and the way she felt, she said that she was worried you were going to wind up as a kind of victim of whatever this pattern may be."

Gene put down his plate and lit another cigarette. He decided he'd had enough of Walter Farlowe's cooking. "Did she give you any indication of what this pattern was?" he asked.

Peter Graves shrugged. "She knows, but she's not telling."

"Are you sure of that?"

"Absolutely. I've seen it before. There's some part of her personality that she is consciously sublimating to the point where it's almost impossible for any analyst to reach. That lady of yours has a mental brick wall around her real personality that's almost impenetrable."

Gene blew out smoke. "*Almost* impenetrable?"

Peter nodded. "The only way to get through it, the only way to discover what she's hiding and why she's hiding it, is to trigger off the predestined fate she keeps talking about."

"I don't get that," said Gene, frowning.

"Well, you said she'd told you to swear not to marry her, right? That was an effort on her part to avoid this predestined fate, But if you *were* to ask her to marry you, and you *did* get married, then I guess that would be a trigger for the traditional pattern, and she would have to go through the whole rigmarole, and expose that part of her personality that she's been trying to hide."

"That sounds pretty hypothetical," Gene said.

Peter swallowed some 7-Up, and suppressed a burp. "Not at all. What a lot of people don't seem to realize these days is that basic psychiatry is like practical mechanics. Your Lorie is a completely predictable and straightforward example of anxiety. Because of some past situation in her life, she believes that if she takes a particular course of action, something awful is going to happen, and therefore she avoids that course at all costs. To get her out of the anxiety, she needs someone to show her that it's not necessarily going to be that way."

"You mean, I ought to ask her to marry me?"

Peter scratched the back of his neck. "That would be the ideal solution, yes. But obviously you mustn't do it unless you mean it."

Gene said nothing. He looked across the still, reflecting pool to where Lorie stood, laughing politely with the other women, and she was so tempting in her safari suit, with her gleaming gold hair and her slanted green eyes, that he wondered how any man could possibly resist her. He wanted her, almost desperately, and he was beginning to wonder if asking her to marry him wasn't the only way.

That evening, as a smoldering crimson sun sank behind the hills in a grayish haze, they left Walter Farlowe's place and drove back to Washington. Gene had drunk three too many vodkatinis, and wasn't driving very straight, but Lorie was too high and happy to notice. Their date had opened her out like a Japanese paper flower in water, and she was chattering about all the people she was going to meet and all the things she was going to do.

"Did you have a good time?" asked Gene. He knew she had, but he just wanted to hear her say it.

"Oh, Gene, it was *fantastic.* You know, I've kept myself bottled up for so many years, and I've never wanted to get out and talk to people but now that I have, I love it. I could go to a party every night."

"Your father was pretty sociable, wasn't he, from what I've heard?"

She nodded. "He was the best host in Washington. Mother has an album about him upstairs, and it's full of newspaper cuttings about his dances and his parties."

Gene lit a cigarette. "That was pretty sad, what happened to him."

"Yes," she said quietly. "I miss him."

"Does your mother ever think about remarriage?"

Lorie brushed back her hair with her hand. "Oh, no."

"You seem very certain of that."

"It's the way our people are. It's traditional that a woman has only one man in her lifetime, and I don't think that Mother could ever consider anyone else. She believes too much in the old customs."

"It seems a pity. She's an attractive woman. If I wasn't going out with you, I could almost fancy her myself."

"Now then," laughed Lorie. "You'll make me jealous."

He shook his head. "You have nothing to be jealous about, ever. You have everything going for you that any girl ever could. You're truly a beautiful person, you know that?"

She looked away. Her tawny hair shone in the last reddish light of the sinking sun.

"You mustn't get too serious," she said.

"Who's talking about serious? Can't we have some fun together?"

She turned around, and gave a fleeting, preoccupied smile. "I guess so. It's just that I don't want you to think that we can ever get any closer."

He looked across at her and sighed. Talking to her

about love was like fencing with an opponent who was ten moves ahead at every stroke. Parry, riposte, lunge. No matter how he angled his conversation, she was always moving away, always defensive, carrying her secret so close that he couldn't even guess what it was.

He flicked his cigarette out of the window.

"Do you think you're ever going to be totally honest with me?" he said. "I mean, are you ever going to tell me what it is that's bugging you?"

She was silent for a moment. "It's no use, Gene," she said. "I can't tell you anything. Believe me, it's better this way."

"How *can* it be better if it's driving me nuts? What is it with you? What can you have possibly done that makes it out of the question for us to get married? Have you been in jail? In a mental hospital? Is there something wrong with your chromosomes? I just can't imagine anything that puts marriage beyond the pale."

Again, she didn't answer for a long time. But eventually she said: "The people of Ubasti are . . . different, that's all."

"You mean like Amish?"

"In a way. Some of the difference is religious."

"So, if I wanted to marry you, I could change my religion. So I'm Protestant. What's to stop me converting to whatever it is—Ubasti?"

"No. You could never be Ubasti."

He followed the overhead traffic signs that directed him toward the city center. It was almost dark now, and cars were flashing past in blurs of white and scarlet light.

"To tell you the truth," he said, "I never heard of Ubasti. That's a terrible admission for someone from the State Department, but I have to confess it."

Lorie said nothing. He glanced across at her again,

but he had the distinct impression that she didn't want to talk about her religion or her race, and that the conversation was closed.

They drove another twenty minutes in silence, and then Lorie said, "That was the Merriam exit back there. You just missed it."

"I know. I thought we'd go back to my place for a nightcap. You don't mind that, do you? I'm not going to propose."

She appeared to be anxious. "I did tell mother that I'd come back before ten."

"It's only a quarter of eight now. We've got plenty of time."

"Really, Gene, I'd rather——"

He raised his hand. "This time we're going to do what *I* want to do. We'll go back and mix ourselves a nice, cold jug of vodka martinis, and then I can rustle up some hamburgers and salad, and we can play Mozart and talk about us."

"Couldn't I just drop by and tell mother I'm going to be late?"

"Forget mother," he told her. "You're twenty years old and beautiful and the night is still young."

"But——"

"Forget her. That's an order from an important government executive."

Lorie finally smiled. "All right, Mister Executive. I surrender. I'm just glad I don't have to argue diplomacy with you over the conference table. I might lose."

He grinned. "Lorie, you'll never lose. Not to me. Not to anyone. It's about time you untied your mother's apron strings and started to realize that you're a winner."

When they arrived back at Gene's apartment, he showed her where the kitchen was and asked her to get the hamburger meat out of the icebox while he mixed the vodka. It was a neat, modern kitchen with hardwood worktops and bright orange cupboards. Lorie poked around looking for plates, spice jars, and cutlery while Gene filled a glass jug with ice and went to the sitting room to fix the drinks.

"It must be wonderful, having your own apartment in the center of the city," she called.

"It suits me," said Gene.

He finished mixing the vodka and went back into the kitchen. Lorie was laying everything out, and heating up the grill to cook the hamburgers. He stood behind her, and put his arms around her, nuzzling her hair with his face.

She went suddenly tense.

"Gene," she said, "don't hold me like that."

He kissed her. "Why not? I'm enjoying it."

"Please," she insisted. "Don't hold me!"

He backed off, feeling snubbed. "I was just trying to be affectionate. Is affection a crime? Or is it against your religion?"

"Gene, I'm sorry, but when you touch me it makes me nervous."

"Listen, it makes *me* nervous as well, but it's a *nice* nervous."

She turned and faced him. She was tall and gracious, and when she looked at him that way he knew how much he wanted her. Her eyes were glowing green, and her lips were glossy in the fluorescent light of the kitchen. Her big breasts softly stretched the front of her safari jacket, and her long legs were tightly outlined in brown leather boots. And all the time there was that faint lingering scent about her, that musky scent that aroused him more than he could ever remember being aroused before.

"Gene," she said simply. "You know how much I like you."

"It's okay," he replied. "It's absolutely okay. If you don't want to rush things, I'm not going to force you."

"Gene, it's not that at all."

He leaned against the kitchen cupboards and gave her a sour little girn. "It doesn't matter what it is, does it? You're as nervous as a cat. The best thing for you to do is relax, and have a drink, and when you feel like it, it will all happen so naturally you won't even think about it."

She looked away from him.

"Come on," he said, "why don't you fix us a couple of Semple burgers and we can talk about it like mature, responsible adults."

"All right," she whispered. "I'm sorry."

He leaned forward, and reluctantly she bent her head so that he could kiss her on the forehead.

"It's not that I'm . . . well, I'm not frigid or anything," she said quickly. "You mustn't think that I don't find you attractive. I do. I think you're very attractive."

"It's okay," he insisted. "You don't have to qualify yourself."

She took his hand and held it close between hers. "Please understand that I've never been out with a man on my own before, except for my father, and that I've never taken off my clothes in front of anyone."

"I understand," he said simply. "Now, how about some dinner?"

"Yes," she said, smiling, and he lifted her hands to his lips and kissed them. Then he went into the sitting room to pour some drinks while she busied herself with the meal. She found eggs in the icebox and onions in the vegetable cupboard, and she clattered around with spoons and basins while Gene sat down in his big leather armchair and watched Superbowl football without the sound.

"I bet you're a fantastic cook," Gene called out.

She laughed. "Wait until you've tasted these hamburgers first."

There was a heavy tussle going on at the eight-yard line, and Gene tried to figure out who was doing what to whom as he sipped his chilly cocktail and relaxed his tired muscles. He had enjoyed Walter Farlowe's cook-out, despite the charcoaled steaks, but after making light and witty conversation to doctors and bankers and flirting, middle-aged ladies all afternoon, he was glad to sit back and let his tensions seep out of his mind and his body on an ebb tide of television and vodka.

"I'm starving," he said. "The quicker you can rustle up those burgers, the better."

He watched the ball being cleared, and he could see the Superbowl crowd silently cheering and waving their arms. It was only after two or three minutes that he realized the kitchen had gone quiet, and that Lorie was no longer whisking or frying or whatever she'd been doing before. He pricked up his ears but all he could hear was Mozart. "Lorie?" he said.

Frowning, he set down his drink and got up from his chair. He walked quietly across the sitting room to the half-open kitchen door, and laid his hand on the knob. He was just about to open it wide when he heard a noise that made him pause. It was a kind of snuffling, gnawing noise. He listened to it for a while, and then stepped quietly back and put his eye to the crack in the door.

What he saw gave him a freezing feeling all the way down his back. Lorie was standing in the middle of the kitchen with a huge handful of raw, unseasoned hamburger meat, and she was craming it into her mouth so that the blood stained her chin and ran between her fingers. Her eyes were closed, and the expression on her face was that of a fierce animal devouring its prey.

Four

For one horrified moment, he was tempted to push open the door and confront her. But then she laid the half-eaten meat down on the kitchen counter and wiped her mouth with the back of her hand, and he knew that if he surprised her and told her that he knew what she'd done, he was going to foul up any chance he ever had of getting to know her better.

Whatever her secret was—whatever psychological problem caused her to keep her body and personality as tightly closed as her kisses—he would never persuade her to relax if he forced a showdown. As Peter Graves had said, Lorie believed that her life was overshadowed by some threatening predestined fate, and the only way to convince her that it wasn't so frightening was to go along with it, and take it to its ultimate conclusion.

Apart from that, what was really so weird about eating raw meat? He ate steak tartare himself, and he guessed that maybe Egyptain people had unusual tastes in food.

He retreated slowly back across the sitting room, and picked up his drink. He was thoughtful as he sipped the ice-cold vodka, but he wasn't quite so disturbed. The Mozart record came to an end, and as the stylus lifted itself gently off the record, he heard the sputtering sound of grilling burgers. He shook his head and mentally rapped his own knuckle for being so easily shocked, and went to put on Debussy.

"How are you doing in there?" he called out. "Do you want any help?"

There was a pause. "No thanks. I'm just making the salad. I won't be long."

Gene sat down and stretched his legs. Ever since Peter had talked about Lorie's personality problems during the afternoon, and suggested that marriage might be one way of getting her out of them, he had been turning over the idea of matrimony, and trying to work out what he felt about it. If anyone had told him a couple of weeks ago that he would soon be considering marriage, he would have laughed in their face. But right now there was a voice inside him that kept asking, "Why not? She's beautiful, she's classy, she's the daughter of a foreign diplomat. Do you really think you're ever going to find anyone better suited to take on the privileged role of being Mrs. Gene Keiller? He even said the name Lorie Keiller under his breath, and it sounded good.

The kitcnen door swung open and Lorie came in with a tray. He couldn't help glancing at her mouth to see if there were any traces of raw blood, but she looked just as sensual and gorgeous as always, and she gave him a radiant smile when she sat down beside him that dissolved all of his chilly tensions.

He lifted the bun of his hamburger and looked at the meat.

"This is kind of a small one. I thought I had more meat than that."

Lorie helped him to fresh salad—tomatoes, onions and crisp lettuce.

"I'm sorry," she said calmly. "That's all there was."

He shrugged. "That's okay. I have to watch my waistline anyway."

They listened to music and ate, and when their meal was finished Lorie took out the tray and washed up. While she was drying the dishes, Gene lowered the lights in the sitting-room to a romantic darkness, and poured her another drink. He wasn't at all sure how far he was going to get with her, but his motto had always been that if you don't try, you never even give yourself the chance.

When she came out of the kitchen, he handed her the vodkatini. "That's the end of your household duties for today. Come and sit down."

"I mustn't stay too long. I don't want Mother to worry."

He patted the settee beside him. "Sit down! And stop fretting about your mother. How do you think she met your father and had you? By going home early to Grandma?"

Lorie sat down. Her hair shone dimly in the lamplight, and her lips gleamed as if she'd been licking them. It was warm in Gene's apartment, and she'd unbuttoned her safari jacket a little so that he could see her deep cleavage and the tiny gold spark of her pyramid pendant. She sat quite close, and he breathed in her perfume and the sheer bodily heat she radiated, and he was convinced, then and there, that he loved her.

"My mother met my father at Tell Besta, in Egypt," she said. "It's in ruins now, but that's where our people originally came from."

"You mean recent ruins or ancient ruins?"

"Ancient," she said. "Even more ancient than the pyramids. Even older than the Sphinx herself."

He reached over and opened his cigarette box. "So

you come from a pretty long line of what's-its-names? Ubastis?"

She nodded. "The city of Tell Besta, where our people used to live, was once called Bubastis, and it was supposed to have been at its greatest in the days of Rameses III."

He lit a True and blew out smoke. "And you can trace your family back to there?"

She nodded again.

"And how long ago was he—Rameses III? I'm afraid my ancient Egyptian history isn't very good."

She sipped her drink. "The reign of Rameses III was one thousand three hundred years before the birth of Christ."

Gene widened his eyes. "You're kidding! You mean you can trace your ancestors back to thirteen hundred BC? That's incredible!"

She smiled gently. "It's not really. The people in that part of lower Egypt were never nomadic. There are many fellaheen with extraordinary faces that look just like the drawings on the walls of ancient tombs. But it's not surprising when you think that they are direct descendants of the same people who made those tombs, and because there is a great deal of inbreeding, with cousins marrying cousins, and even brothers marrying sisters, the facial characteristics have remained constant for thousands of years."

Gene sat back. "You know something," he said, "I can trace my family back to a Scotsman who emigrated to Florida in 1825, and I used to be proud of that. You make me feel like I don't have any lineage at all."

She lowered her eyes. "A long lineage is not necessarily a good lineage," she said, very quietly.

"You're telling me there's something wrong with tracing your family back so far?"

Lorie looked at him. "It depends on who, and what your family was. My ancestors were not particularly liked. The fellaheen used to call them 'that people.' I think they still do."

" 'That people?' That doesn't sound so bad."

"It does when you realize that the fellaheen are masters of the insult and the epithet," she said. "They can curse you for an hour and never call you the same thing twice. But our people, the Ubasti, they call nothing but 'that people,' and that is the highest expression of their feelings about us they are capable of devising."

Gene reached over and touched her hair. It was soft and fine, but it had a wiry strength all its own, and in the subdued light of the apartment it took on a golden hue that reminded him of something he couldn't quite bring to mind.

"We have the same kind of feuding in America," he told her. "Did you ever hear of the Hatfields and the McCoys?"

"Yes," she said, "but it was nothing like that. It had nothing to do with feuding. It was fear."

"Fear? Were your ancestors that bad?"

He was caressing her cheek now with the back of his fingers, and she fixed her glittering green eyes on him intently. The pupils had widened in the darkness, and he never once saw her blink. He became aware of some inner tightening inside her that she was trying hard to conceal, but as they talked more and more it became increasingly obvious that she was sitting there with every muscle in her body compressed with latent energy. She's not looking at me, she's *watching* me, he thought. She's watching every single insignificant move I make.

"I shouldn't really talk about my ancestors like

that," she told him. "Even if they've been dead for two thousand years, it's still disloyal."

"I don't know," he said softly. "You talk like they only died yesterday."

She kept on watching him, and she didn't stir at all.

"That's because we speak about them at home, nearly all the time," she said. Mother doesn't want me to forget my Egyptian background. She likes America, but she doesn't want me to forget."

"And how about you? Would you prefer to forget?"

"No," she said, almost inaudibly. "I cannot prefer to forget. What my ancestors were, and are, is unforgettable."

He soothingly stroked her neck and caressed her ears. Before, when he had touched her, she had resented his touch, but she seemed to find this kind of idle fingerplay soothing. As he ran his hands through her hair, he was conscious that her muscular tightness was gradually easing, and that her eyes, so staring and watchful a few moments ago, were now closing.

"You like that?" he said. He didn't even have to ask.

"That's nice," she murmured, and she stretched herself until the last tensions had flowed from her body and she was utterly relaxed.

"Lorie," he said, as he massaged her scalp, feeling the symmetrical shape of her head in his hand.

Her eyes remained closed. "Umh-humh?"

"Lorie, I'm going to say something real serious."

She was enjoying his sensitive caress so much that she was purring with pleasure.

"Go on, then," she said.

He looked at her distinctive, angular face for a while, and the way her long eyelashes curved from her closed eyes. "I know this sounds kind of crazy. I didn't think it could happen myself. I'm in politics, you know? And that makes most people cynical. But I have to face up to the fact that it's true, and because it's true I know that I'm going to have to come out with it tonight, or tomorrow night, or some night, well, it might just as well be tonight."

She was purring loudly now, rubbing her head back against his hand so that he could stroke her ears.

"Lorie," he said softly. "I love you."

There was a pause. She stopped rubbing against him, and her slanting eyes gradually opened. He looked at her as sincerely and strongly as he could, because he wanted her to see from his expression alone that he meant what he said.

"You . . . love me?"

"Yes," he whispered.

Her eyes flickered away from him. A slight worried crease marked her forehead.

"Gene," she said, "you mustn't!"

He sat up. "What do you mean, 'mustn't?' It's not a question of 'mustn't!' I don't have any choice in the matter. I've fallen in love with you whether you like it or not!"

"Gene . . ."

"No," he said bluntly. "This time, I don't want any excuses! We've been through all this mysterious rigmarole of why I must never ask you to marry me, and why I shouldn't love you, and it's wearing thin. If you're afraid of something, why don't you come out straight and tell me? I'm a grown man, Lorie. I'm old enough to know what I want, and what I want is *you*, whether you've been jailed or raped or treated for mental sickness or whatever it is."

Her eyes opened wide. "You think that I was raped? Or locked up in jail? Gene, I don't understand!"

He stood up and paced tautly across the carpet. "Lorie," he said "I just didn't know *what* to think. All I knew was that I fancied you like crazy, and that you appeared to fancy me, too, and yet whenever it looked like we might do something that normal people do when they fancy each other, like kiss or go out for dinner, you clammed up tight and told me to move along."

He sat down beside her again and held her hands. "I know that you've led a sheltered life, and I know it's difficult for you to form any kind of relationship. But you're twenty years old, and you're beautiful, and you can't stay in your ivory tower forever. Some day, sooner or later, you're going to want to form a permanent lifetime association with somebody, whether it's marriage or not, and you can't go on hiding behind these adolescent fantasies."

She looked confused. "Fantasies? I don't know what you mean."

He sighed. "Come on, Lorie, every young girl does it. She goes out with a man for the first time, and she's worried that she's not sophisticated enough, or mysterious enough. So she uses her imagination. A hint of mystique here, a touch of melodrama there. When I was fifteen I dated a girl of thirteen who told me her father was once a famous concert pianist. According to her, he had burned his hands beyond recovery by rescuing her from a fire. It turned out the poor stiff worked in a bakery, and his only musical talent was whistling 'After the Ball Is Over.' "

Lorie listened to this, and sat there silently for a long time. "Gene," she said, "don't you think we'd better make this the first and last date?"

"You've decided you don't like me, huh? Is that it?"

"No, that's not it."

"Then you *do* like me?"

"Yes. And that's the trouble."

Gene reached out again and stroked her cheek. She looked desperately sad, and he wished to God he knew why. She held his hand in hers and pressed it against her lips, kissing it gently.

"The truth is, Gene, that I love you, too."

He couldn't quite believe what he'd heard. "Are you kidding me? By Christ, Lorie, I hope you're not kidding me."

"It's true," she said, in a throaty voice. "I think they call it love at first sight."

He gave her a small, wry smile. "More like love at first *bite,* if you ask me."

She lifted her head. Her eyes were brimming with tears she didn't want to cry, and she couldn't help sniffing.

"I loved you the first time I saw you," she said. "I know I haven't dated any other men, and that I don't have any experience. Maybe I'm childish when it comes to love. But that's just the way I am, and you're going to have to accept it. I love you, Gene, and that's all I can say. I love you more than anything."

"Lorie," he whispered. He held her close, and he kissed her. "Lorie why the hell didn't you say . . . ?"

She started weeping openly now. "I couldn't say because it can't last. It can't happen. I can't *allow* it to happen. If I fall in love with you, then it's all going to start all over again, and I couldn't stand it."

He took a handkerchief out of his pocket and dabbed at her tears. "You're still talking mysteries," he told her. "What can't you allow to happen? What's going to start all over again?"

She blew her nose. "I can't tell you," she said. "Not now, nor ever."

He took another cigarette out of the box and lit it. He took a long deep drag to steady his nerves. "Not ever? Not even if we got married?"

She stared at him, her face pale and her eyes blotted with tears.

"Please, Gene," she said. "You swore you'd never ask. You swore."

He tried to manage a smile, but it came out unsteady and lopsided. "I'm a politician, remember? Politicians have divine dispensation to break promises."

He tried to call her again and again on Monday, but the phone rang hollow and distant and nobody answered. An unhelpful receptionist at the Franco-African Bank said that Lorie Semple hadn't arrived for work and he didn't have the time to go there and check for himself. Henry Ness wanted a detailed profile of political structures on three Caribbean islands, and he spent an irritating morning collecting data and statistics on banana production and sugar shipping.

He had taken Lorie home on Saturday night, late, and they had kissed, but the date had ended inconclusively, and he wasn't even sure if he was ever going to see her again. She refused to talk about marriage and she refused to discuss love, and she couldn't say when she might have another free evening. In the end, he had driven off with a furiously surpressed temper and hadn't simmered down until he got home and finished the left over jug of vodka.

"Walter's looking for you," Maggie said." He's not very happy about the Isthmus file."

Gene lit his fifteenth cigarette of the day and refused to look up. "If Walter's unhappy about the Isthmus file, let Walter come 'round here himself and tell me."

"What is this?" asked Maggie. "The workers revolution?"

"No," he said bluntly, "it's just the first day of Keep Your Nose Out Week."

Maggie glanced at the stack of untidy files on his desk. "Sugar's sweet but Lorie isn't—is that it?"

He scribbled percentages in the margin of his notepad. "Something like that. It's a mystery of the first magnitude, if you must know."

"I don't getcha."

He sat back in his swivel chair and stretched. Outside, through the pale-green Venetian blinds, it looked as if a dark thunderstorm was looming from the west. It was only one-thirty, but they had switched on all the office lights, and there was a humid electricity in the air that didn't do anything to make him feel better.

"I'm totally baffled, if you must know," he said patiently. "She says she loves me, but she doesn't want to be hugged, she's reluctant to kiss, and she won't even make arrangements for another date. I ask her why, and she goes into histrionics and says there's some kind of mysterious reason that she can't explain."

"Do you like her that much?" Maggie asked.

"What do you mean?"

"I mean, do you like her enough to take that kind of stuff?"

He shook his head. "I don't know. I like her a lot. I love her, I think."

"Oh."

Gene saw Maggie's disappointed expression. "Come on, Maggie, he said. "It's got to happen sooner or later. You said so yourself."

"I know that. I just don't want you to get hurt."

"Maggie, I'm thirty-two."

"So you keep telling me. Eight years to go till you're

forty. Too young to settle down but too old to get hurt."

Gene couldn't help laughing. "Get out of here before I marry you," he joked.

Maggie was leaving when his telephone rang. He picked it up. "Mr. Keiller? There's a call for you," the switchboard girl said. "Sounds like someone called Sumpler."

Semple, pronounced with a heavy French accent. The way that Lorie's mother spoke.

"Okay," said Gene uncertainly. "Put her through."

When Mrs. Semple spoke, she seemed curiously close, as if she was standing right next to him and whispering in his ear. Her voice was rich and vibrant, and she sounded as intimate and confiding as his own mother.

"Gene? How is your shoulder?"

"Hi, Mrs. Semple. It's fine, thanks. You did a beautiful sewing-up job there. I don't know why you didn't become a professional surgeon."

"It was something I picked up from an old Turkish doctor in Zagazig. Nothing special, I'm afraid. You may always have a scar."

"I expect I can live with it. How's Lorie?"

"Lorie is very well."

"She's not at work."

"Oh, you called the bank. No, well, she's a little tired, but otherwise she's fine. It was about Lorie that I rang you, as a matter of fact."

He crushed out his cigarette in his Democratic souvenir ashtray and waited to hear the worst. Perhaps Lorie had asked her mother to call him and put him off for good. Well, he'd been expecting it. He was beginning to think that his brief encounter with Lorie Semple was going to be just that and nothing more. A tantalizing image that faded on the retina almost as soon as you looked at it.

"Gene, I want to ask you a question," Mrs. Semple said.

"Go ahead. What do you want to know?"

"I want to know if you suggested to Lorie that you might marry her."

Gene took a deep breath. "Let's put it this way, Mrs. Semple. The subject did come up. Very prematurely, I admit, and probably foolishly, but it did come up."

"And Lorie said no?"

"That seems to be her prevailing attitude, yes."

"I love the way you politicians talk."

"We go to a special school of political double-talk, actually. Is that it?"

"Is what it?"

"Is that all you called me to say?"

"*Non, non*, not at all. I called to say that she says yes."

Gene rubbed his eyes. "I'm sorry, I don't quite follow."

"Lorie says yes," said Mrs. Semple. "I had a long discussion with her, and now she says yes."

"You mean——"

"Of course, I mean she will marry you!"

Gene took the receiver away from his ear and stared at it. "What is it? What's happened? Have they assassinated Henry?" Maggie asked, standing by the door.

Gene ignored her. He put the phone back against his ear. "Mrs. Semple, I don't get it."

"There is nothing to get," said Mrs. Semple happily. "She loves you, and she wants to marry you."

"But she seemed so worried before. She kept saying

that she was afraid something was going to happen all over again, and I couldn't understand what."

"Merely a young girl's imagination," said Mrs. Semple, deprecatingly. "The only thing that matters is that she adores you and wants to spend the rest of your life with you."

"Mrs. Semple, this is all very sudden."

"Ahh," cooed Mrs. Semple, "but isn't that the way of everything? We are suddenly conceived, we are suddenly born, and we suddenly die."

"Yes," said Gene, "I suppose we do."

He still looked distinctly unsettled when he laid the phone down, and Maggie saw him gazing at it for a long time afterward, as if he almost expected it to jump across his desk and bite him.

They were married quietly in Merriam on an unseasonably warm day three weeks later. All of the wedding guests, with the exception of the silent Mathieu and the elegant Mrs. Semple, were friends of Gene's. There was a simple ceremony in the white-painted church that stood a little way down the hill from the Semple mansion, everyone threw confetti on the church steps, a photographer took pictures for *The Washington Post,* and Maggie stood on her own amongst the ankle-deep leaves of fall and cried.

The reception was held at a colonial-style tavern overlooking the Potomac, and all the young men from Gene's office came up and whispered in his ear what a lucky bastard he was and clustered around Mrs. Semple in callow admiration. As Walter Farlowe said, after too many glasses of Heidsieck champagne, "You may not have married into money, but you sure married into tits."

Lorie wore a wedding dress of white silk with a

white lace overlay and looked glowing and beautiful and happy. She stayed close to Gene all day, and even though he felt slightly amazed and unreal, he knew, in a curiously dogmatic way, that he was elated and pleased. He kissed his bride over and over, and when the last of the guests had left he sat with her at the window of the tavern with a glass of champagne, looking down at the slow-moving river and holding her close.

"I'm going to tell you something," he said. "This is the happiest day of my whole life."

She leaned her head against him. "I know," she said quietly.

He swallowed champagne. "Maybe, one day, we'll take our children down here, show them the river, and say that—"

She tugged her arm away. He looked up and realized she was worried and upset. "What is it? What's the matter?" Gene asked.

"It's nothing," she said, attempting to smile.

"Oh, come on, Lorie. There's no room for any kind of mystery now. We're married. You're my wife. If there's something upsetting you, I want to know what it is."

She bent forward and kissed him. Her cheeks were flushed with excitement and champagne. "It's really nothing," she told him. "I think I'm tired, that's all. I'd like to get changed and have a rest. It's been one of those fantastic days that leaves you absolutely exhausted."

"Okay. Let's get back to the house. Will Mathieu drive us?"

They left the tavern and went outside. In the graveled car park, Mathieu was waiting silently and impassively at the wheel of the black Fleetwood, and when he saw them he climbed out and opened the rear door. Lorie got into the car, but Gene paused for a moment. "Mathieu," he said. "I hope you and I can be friends."

Mathieu, behind reflecting sunglasses that showed nothing but Gene's own distorted, anxious face, neither moved nor signaled with his hands that he had understood. He stood stolidly waiting for Gene to get into the car, and then he shut the door. He slid into the driver's seat, started the engine, and they glided away.

Because Gene was hard-pressed by political commitments, they had decided to spend the first few weeks of their married life at the Semple mansion. Then, as soon as it looked as though the Caribbean situation was easing up a little, they were going to take a two-week skiing vacation and then look for a house of their own, close to Washington. But, as Mrs. Semple had said, "You can stay here as long as you like. This place is big enough for you, and me, and even my darling little granddaughter."

"I'm counting on a son first," Gene had said, but Mrs. Semple had only laughed. He had the strangest feeling that she *knew*, or at least *believed* she knew, that their first baby was going to be a girl.

They drove along the avenue of oaks, and rolled up outside the Semple mansion with a soft crunch of tires on gravel. Mathieu opened the doors for them, and they stepped out. The house was still dark and forbidding to Gene, but he guessed he was going to have to get used to it. They went through the pillared portico into the large and gloomy hallway, which was hung with African spears and shields and foxed etchings of water-buffalo. A black oak staircase rose up on one side of the hall to the upper floor, and a stained-glass window allowed a strain of colored light to fall across the landing and illuminate the walls.

"I think I'm going to carry you over the threshold," announced Gene. He bent his knees, and tried to lift Lorie off the floor. Straining, he managed to raise her about five or six inches, but then he suddenly realized that he wasn't going to be able to make it. She was a tall girl, yes, but he hadn't realized how *heavy* she was. It was like trying to lift a huge, floppy, uncooperative animal.

Panting, he laid her carefully down again. "Mrs. Keiller," he said, "I'm afraid this is one threshold you're going to have to walk over by yourself. It looks like I'm going to have to do some physical shaping-up before we buy our new home."

Lorie laughed. "I thought I married an ace politician and it looks like I've married a 126-pound weakling."

"I'll have you know I weigh one-hundred-ninety-two, and that's without two slices of wedding-cake."

Mathieu went ahead of them, carrying Gene's cases along the landing, past the stained-glass window, to a dark oak door at the end of the upstairs corridor. It was right next to the small bedroom where Gene had recuperated after his brush with the guard dogs. Mathieu unlocked the door and let them in.

"This room's beautiful," Gene said. "Look at that bed! This is really terrific."

In the center of the facing wall was a high four-poster bed, with carved mahogany pillars and a magnificent headboard depicting wild animals roaming through leaves and flowers. It was covered in a bedspread made of zebra-skins.

The room around it was painted a pale primrose color, with a darker, gold carpet, and the furniture was all French antique, pieces from various châteaux. Mrs. Semple had filled it with fresh flowers flown in from Florida, and the fragrance was almost overwhelming.

Mathieu laid down the cases and went to open the drapes. The room was on the south-east corner of the house, so that it caught the rising sun, and it had a magnificent view over the trees and fields of the Semple estate.

Gene went to the window to look out, but he became aware that Mathieu was still standing in the room, as still as a waxwork, as if he was waiting for something.

"Oh, I'm sorry," said Gene, fumbling in his pocket for a ten-dollar bill. "Here, take this, and thanks a lot."

Mathieu didn't move. He didn't raise his hand to take the money, or even to indicate that he didn't want it.

Suddenly he spoke, in that hoarse, laborious, unnatural voice that people use when their larynxes have been removed by surgeons.

"Smith's gazelle," he said, croakily.

Gene frowned, and turned to Lorie.

"What does he mean?" he asked her. "Mathieu, what are you trying to say?"

Lorie stepped forward and put her arm around Mathieu's shoulder. She smiled at him, and stroked his epaulette.

"I don't think Mathieu meant anything, darling. Did you, Mathieu? It's just his little joke."

Mathieu paused for a moment. Lorie said, "Mathieu, that will be all," the chauffeur put on his cap, and turned around, and walked out of the room, closing the door behind him with a firm and final click.

"I'm sure he said 'Smith's gazelle,'" said Gene. "Isn't that some kind of African antelope?"

"Oh, don't worry about him," said Lorie, pulling away her white veil. "I think all that torture in Algeria turned his brain. He's usually lucid, but he does come out with some very odd things."

Gene walked over and put his arms around her. "Well," he said warmly. "What does it feel like to be Mrs. Kieller?"

She coquettishly put her head on one side. "It's a little strange," she admitted. "I think it's going to take me a little while to get used to it. I've been Lorie Semple for twenty years, you know, and I've only been Lorie Keiller for twenty minutes."

"Your mother won't be back for half-an-hour," he grinned, reaching behind her and unfastening the top button of her wedding-dress.

She twisted away from him. "Half-an-hour isn't long," she protested. "Supposing she comes upstairs and finds that we're——"

He went after her, and held her close. "Well, then," he said, kissing her, "we'll lock the door."

Lorie looked at him with her green, liquid eyes. "She might look through the keyhole."

Gene just nodded, and smiled, and said, "Yes, she might," and reached for the second button.

Lorie tensed. She reached up and held his wrists. "Please, Gene, not now. Wait till this evening."

"But what *for*?" he said, feeling irritated but trying to sounding reasonable. "We're married now. All the social conventions have been observed. If we don't do it now, our marriage will be unconsummated until the sun goes down, and at Florida State U. that was considered to be extremely bad luck."

"It's just . . . I'd rather not," said Lorie, turning away.

Gene reached out and took hold of her hand. It was completely limp and unresponsive, and a terrible sick feeling went through him that perhaps, after all, he had actually married a frigid woman. Why else was she so reluctant to make love? Why else had she tried to stop him from marrying her? Why else was a girl as beautiful as Lorie still a virgin on her wedding night?

"Lorie," he said huskily, "are you sure you're feeling okay?"

"I'm . . . fine," she told him. She was hypertense and white-faced, and a kind of nervous shudder went through her that made him think she must be sickening for something, or in a mild state of hysteria.

"Do you feel sick?" he asked her.

"Sick?" she said, abstractedly. "No, I'm not sick. I feel hungry. I could really eat something. For some reason, right now, I'm absolutely ravenous. Maybe I'll just go downstairs to the kitchen and get myself something."

Gene walked over to the window and lit a cigarette. "Maybe you won't go downstairs," he said quietly. "Maybe you'll stay right here and tell me what's wrong."

"There's nothing wrong. I don't know what you mean."

Gene turned around to face her. "Lorie," he said, "we just got married."

"Yes," she said, "I know."

He spread his arms in exasperation. "Doesn't that mean anything to you? We're man and wife. We're supposed to be passionately in love with each other. We're supposed to fling ourselves on the bed and have mad, crazy, delirious intercourse. Instead, you want to go downstairs and raid the icebox. What's it going to be? A pound of raw steak?"

Lorie's eyes widened.

"I'm sorry," said Gene, "but I've been looking forward to this and now I'm disappointed. I'm frustrated, too. You're my wife, I love you, and I haven't seen you naked yet."

She lowered her eyes, and in the warm sunlight she was classically and perfectly beautiful—a white virgin madonna in a virginal white dress.

"Gene," she whispered, "you must never see me naked."

He stared at her. Some cigarette smoke went down the wrong way, and he coughed.

"I beg your pardon," he said. "I could have sworn you said I could never see you naked."

She nodded.

He bent his head thoughtfully for a moment, and then he leaned over and crushed his cigarette out in a small procelain ashtray. He shucked off the gray coat of his morning suit, and walked across to Lorie in his formal white shirt and gray pants.

"Take off that dress," he said, in a soft voice.

Lorie lifted her proud head. "Gene, I'm sorry, I can't."

"Do you have a reason?" he asked her.

She nodded dumbly.

"What is the reason."

She shook her head.

"You're not going to tell me?"

She shook her head again.

"In that case," he said, "I'm going to tear the goddamned thing right off you, shred by shred."

"Gene—it's my wedding dress!"

He turned around and banged his fist on the top of the mahogany dresser so that the perfume bottles rattled and a hairbrush dropped on to the floor.

"Lorie, I *know* it's your goddamn wedding dress! Do you think that I *want* to tear it? Why the hell can't you take it off? Why don't you just take some pride in yourself and show your husband your goddamn body?"

"Because I can't, and I can't tell you why! I'm *different*, Gene, you don't understand!"

Gene rubbed the back of his neck in anger and frustration. He took a few deep breaths to try and control himself. "Lorie, I know you're different," he said in a steady and leadenly patient voice. "I married you *because* you're different. You're unlike every other girl I ever knew. You're stunningly attractive, you have a desirable body, and you turn everyone's heads when you walk into a room. Don't you understand that it was *because* you're different that I wanted you?"

She was crying now. Tears ran down her cheeks, and she made no attempt to hide them.

"Gene," she said miserably, "you don't know *how* different."

Without another word, she reached behind her and began to unbutton her wedding dress. He didn't help her, and she cried all the time she was doing it. At last it was undone, and she stepped out of it and laid it on the bed.

Undernaeth, she was wearing white stockings, white suspenders, a short slip and a bra. Her big breasts were firm and shapely, and he could see the pink half-moons of her nipples rising over the white lace of her bra cup.

Gene stood there, aroused and transfixed, but he made no move to undress her, and he didn't say a single word. This was something she had to do for herself. She might never have undressed in front of a man before, but now she was going to have to learn.

She turned her back on him, raised the slip over her head, and then reached behind her to release the bra. He saw her bare breasts swing slightly as she took it off. She wasn't wearing any panties, and her curved and rounded bottom was suntanned the color of freshly poured coffee.

"There," said Gene hoarsely. "Was that so bad?"

She slowly turned around. He was just on the point of walking toward her, his hand half-raised, but what he saw made him stop as suddenly as if he'd been doused in icy-cold water. A terrible feeling of dread and uncertainty swamped over him, and all he could do was stand where he was and stare.

She had beautiful breasts. They were the loveliest breasts he had ever seen, and they were high and tense with youthfulness and crowned with wide, pink nipples. What was different about Lorie, though, was that directly under those breasts she had what looked like the beginnings of another pair of breasts! They were much smaller, like an adolescent girl's, their two pink nipples, were also visible. And, under that pair she had what appeared to be two more nipples, faintly visible, but distinctly breast-like and pink.

Between her thighs grew abundant curls of tawny pubic hair. It formed a fleece that grew right up past her navel, and even grew a few inches down her thighs.

Lorie stood there looking at him her arms wide apart so that he could see everything of her there was to see. She had stopped crying now and she was silent and watchful and proud.

"You see," she said. "I'm different."

Gene picked up his morning coat and groped in the pocket for his cigarettes. He swallowed nervously, and found that he was sweating and shaking with shock.

"W-w-what is it?" he stammered, lighting up his True. "Is it . . . some kind of . . ."

Lorie stalked across the room and stood at the window. "Does it upset you, the fact that I'm like this?" she asked.

He turned away. "I don't know," he breathed uncertainly. "I just didn't imagine that . . ."

She came across and touched his shoulder. He couldn't bear to look at her, in case he found himself staring at those small, unformed breasts under her main breasts, and at that curious and unsettling growth of pubic hair.

"Yes," she said. "It does upset you, doesn't it? I thought it would. That's why I didn't want to show you. At least, if you'd never seen it, you never would have known."

"You really expected me to marry you, and spend the rest of my life with you, without us ever making love?" asked Gene. He couldn't believe what he was hearing, but he couldn't believe what he was seeing, either, and he felt that his life had abruptly and inexplicably taken an extraordinary turn into some maniacal existence that was like a late night horror show on television.

"It could have worked," said Lorie. "You said yourself that playing the field was part of everyday life in Washington. I could have been your chaste and thoughtful escort, and you could have gone out with any girl who took your fancy. I do love you, Gene. You must understand that I really do love you."

Gene sat down. "Jesus Christ," he muttered. "It's like a goddamned nightmare."

Lorie squatted down beside him and stroked his arm soothingly. He smoked for a while, and then said, "Haven't you or your mother ever thought about plastic surgery? I mean, a good plastic surgeon could—"

"Gene," interrupted Lorie, "it's nothing to do with plastic surgery. It's the way we are."

"The way who is?"

"My mother, me, all our ancestors. This is what being Ubasti means.

"It means having six breasts?"

Lori stood up, and went to sit on the end of the bed. She sat in her white stockings and suspenders with her thighs wide apart, and even though he still felt curious tingles of horror in his spine and the back of his hands, he was also aroused by the sight of her.

"American doctors call these 'supplementary breasts,'" said Lorie, cupping her second pair of breasts in her hands. "They're very well chronicled in medical books, and lots of women have more than the usual number of nipples."

Gene dabbed at his sweaty forehead with his handkerchief. He didn't comment on what she'd said, but let her continue.

"For us Ubasti, though," she said, "these breasts are not supplementary, but usual. And it is only because the use of the normal number of six breasts were not properly used by women in the past that they gradually decreased in size, and shrunk, and eventually were bred out of existence altogether. Gene, can you imagine the beauty of a woman with six breasts as big as these?"

Gene looked at her, and shook his head.

"Lorie," he said, "it has to be surgery. You can't spend the rest of your life going around with six nipples. What about swimming in a bikini? And what's going to happen when they take you to the hospital to have our babies? What's the doctor going to say? 'Oh, I suggest you breast-feed, Mrs. Keiller. You've got enough of them.'"

Lorie, unnervingly for Gene, was caressing her own lower nipple. "Can't you see it from my point of view?"

"What about *my* point of view?" demanded Gene.

"You spring it on me after we're married that you're a physical freak, and then you tell me that you don't want to have it corrected!"

She pouted. "You're making me sound completely selfish."

"Well, it's true!" he yelled. "You are completely selfish! I married you on the vague understanding that, under those clothes of yours, you were a beautiful woman! Now I find out that you're overloaded with more breasts than a Dalmatian bitch, and I'm supposed to forget that I'm married to you and play the field? Lorie, what the hell's going through your mind?"

She didn't answer him at all. Instead, she turned and gently said, "At least you won't want to sleep with me now, will you?"

He stopped yelling and stared at her. He got up from his chair, walked across to the bed where she was sitting, and scruitinized her pretty, tempting, confusing, and infuriating face.

"I get the feeling you're actually *pleased*," he told her. "You are, aren't you? You're actually *pleased*."

"Gene," she said, "I've tried to protect you from this from the very start. I've done everything I can."

"You've tried to protect me from what?"

She looked at him with a sad, soft expression. "From yourself, Gene. I tried to warn you so many times but you wouldn't be warned. Whatever I did to put off, you were determined to come blundering into my life without a thought for what I was or anything else. Up until the time you met Mother, I think I could have saved you. But she's too strong for me, Gene. She's my mother, and she's a Ubasti, too. I have to do what she wishes."

"I don't understand a word of this," Gene said.

Lorie brushed back her hair. "Go and look at that

picture next to the dresser," she said. "That's right, that one."

Uncertainly, reluctantly, Gene went over and examined the small, framed etching. It was probably mid-Victorian, judging by the melodrama of what was going on, and the style. It showed a small graceful creature with horns tied up to a stake in the ground. Not far away, huge and powerful and tossing its mane, crouched a lion, ready to pounce on the tiny animal and devour it.

Underneath the etching, an elegantly written caption read, "Smith's gazelle."

Five

They spent a restless night under the gloomy canopy of the four-poster bed. Lorie wore an ankle-length nightdress of pale peach-colored silk, and through the disturbed hours of the early morning, tossing and sighing and trying to relax on wrinkled sheets, Gene made no attempt to touch or hold her.

His feelings were in a scorching turmoil. He knew, somewhere in the middle of that emotional broth, that he still loved Lorie, and that to lose her now would be tragically painful. Now and then he looked across at her as she lay with her eyes closed on the wide, lace-trimmed pillow, and she was just as tempting and tantalizing as she'd always been. But then he thought about her breasts, and the thick hair between her thighs, and he felt his gorge rise in almost total revulsion.

What he couldn't understand was that she was content with her body the way it was. It didn't seem unnatural or ugly to her at all. If anything, she seemed to consider that women with only two breasts were somehow distasteful and inadequate. Gene's mind couldn't get around this acceptance of her own freakishness, any more than a coyote could get its jaws around a whole sheep. Or a Smith's gazelle.

He had been brought up to appreciate American girls on a strictly *Playboy* level. Fresh bouncing hair, wide wholesome smiles, sparkling eyes, and curvy suntanned bodies. In Florida, most of the girls he had dated were like that, with the sole exception of a wan academic young lady he had once taken, out of pity alone, to a John Cage concert. By the time the concert was over the only person he had felt sorry for was himself. To Gene, the ideal of the pretty girl was an indisputable part of the American philosophy of happy living, and it was impossible for him to comprehend anyone who didn't subscribe to it. That didn't mean that he was going to close his mind to Lorie, though. He wasn't that much of a mental stereotype. But it did mean that once he had sorted out her perverse attitude to physical oddity, he was going to do everything he could to get her around to the best plastic surgeon he could afford.

As dawn began to solidify the shadowy images of the night, Lorie stirred, turned over, and reached out to touch his hand. He didn't recoil, although his pulse-rate speeded up, and he found himself waiting tensely for whatever she was going to do.

"Gene," she whispered. "Are you awake?"

He grunted. "I don't think I've slept."

There was a pause, and a rustle of sheets. "I'm sorry, Gene, this was all my fault. I should have told you the truth before."

He coughed. "Well, yes, maybe you should. But it's still not too late, you know. If you want me to go see a doctor I know . . . I mean, I've heard he's an expert on hormones . . . and really I think it's the best thing to do."

"If you like, we could just call it quits. You could get a divorce in Reno, couldn't you? You could say I'd been unfaithful if you wanted to. I'm not after you money."

Gene propped himself up on one elbow. "Lorie," he

said, "I don't get it. Why would you rather walk around with that kind of physical disability than have a short, simple operation and get it over with? You're a beautiful girl, and you could be the most fantastic-looking thing on two legs."

She didn't answer.

"Maybe it'll set us back a few thousand dollars," he continued. "But what's that compared to having a perfect body? I thought every girl wanted to look as gorgeous as possible. I just don't understand you."

She turned her head away. "Gene," she whispered, "it's *me*. This is what I'm like. I'm Ubasti."

He sighed impatiently. Then he swung out of bed, and went across the room to fetch his cigarettes. He normally hated smoking in the bedroom, but he was so wound up that he couldn't stop himself. He lit a cigarette and sat naked in one of the bedside armchairs, blowing smoke into the grainy light of dawn.

"Supposing I told you that, as your husband, I *demand* that you have an operation?" he said.

In the gloom, Lorie's eyes glistened.

"Then I'd have to say no," she said quietly.

"Even though, yesterday, you promised to honor and obey me?"

"Obedience and honor doesn't include changing your hereditary characteristics."

"But they're so goddamn—"

"I know what you think, Gene, and I'm sorry. But it's my own body and I'm proud of it."

She sat up in bed and watched him sadly through the half-light, her arms clasping her knees.

"I love you, Gene," she said gently. "I wanted to marry you right from the start. But I knew what you'd think about me, and all I can say is I'm sorry, and I hope the next girl you find will be better-looking than me."

Gene stubbed out his cigarette. He got up from the chair, went over to the bedroom basin and switched on the light. He washed his face, shaved with his electric razor, and then started to dress. All this time, he didn't look at Lorie once.

"Where are you going?" she asked him, as he laced up his shoes.

He still didn't turn around. "I'm going out," he said, in a controlled and emotionless voice. "I'm not going for good, but I need to think this thing out in my mind. I'll probably be back around nine or ten this evening."

He pulled on his jacket and went to the mirror to straighten his necktie. "Perhaps you'd call Mathieu for me, and get him to kennel the dogs so that I can get out of this place alive."

"Dogs?"

Gene brushed lint from his sleeves. "That's right. Those little pet pooches who practically ripped me to shreds."

"Oh, those," said Lorie absently. "Yes, I'll—"

Gene turned. For some reason, he felt that something was wrong. There was something important about this whole situation that he still didn't know. There was some other secret that Lorie was keeping from him; some hidden knowledge that he sensed was far more terrible than anything he had yet discovered.

Maggie was amazed to see him in the office at ten after eight. "Gene, what happened? Don't tell me the happy husband is *that* anxious to get back to work."

He sat down wearily and looked at her. "Maggie," he said, "I would dearly love a cup of coffee."

As she brought the styrofoam cup from the coffee

machine, he settled back tiredly in his chair and rubbed his eyes. He felt as if he'd been traveling across Siberia all night in a peasant-class train. He sipped the coffee gratefully, then rooted through the drawers of his desk for a spare pack of cigarettes.

Maggie hovered, looking pretty and bright and concerned. He was suddenly so grateful for her presence and her friendship that it brought a lump to his throat. It was probably nothing more than the over-emotional effects of tiredness, but he had to blow his nose to hide his watering eyes.

"Gene," said Maggie, "I wish you'd tell me."

"Well," he told her, dabbing his nose, "there isn't very much to tell. Happily married one minute, and thinking about divorce the next. It must be that shortest marriage in the history of wedlock."

Maggie sat down opposite. "Something awful's happened, hasn't it? What, Gene? Is it something to do with the Semples?"

He nodded. "It certainly is. Listen, before I tell you anything about it, will you trust me for a while and do me a favor?"

"Gene, anything. You know that."

"Go to Records and look up everything you can about a race of people called the Ubasti. They come from a region of lower Egypt near Zagazig, and I think they used to live in a city called Tell something. Tell Bast, or Tell Besta. That was in the reign of Rameses III, about thirteen hundred B.C."

Maggie scribbled the details on her shorthand pad. "The Ubasti?" she said. "Okay, just give me a couple of hours."

"Will you keep it to yourself? I don't want anyone to know what I'm doing until I'm quite certain. There's something . . . strange and wrong about the Semples. I can't work out what it is right now, but I know that it's there, staring me right in the face. I just need more information, that's all."

Maggie laid her hand on top of his, and looked at him with genuine anxiety. "Gene," she said, "what about your marriage? I mean, what's going to happen? Is it really something as wrong and strange as all that?"

He pressed his knuckles to his forehead, and didn't answer her for almost a minute.

"I don't know," he said. "If you can get me that information, then maybe I'll understand enough to do something about it."

"Just two or three hours," she promised. "The Caribbean profiles can wait."

As she folded back the cover of her pad and turned to leave, Gene suddenly thought of something else.

"Maggie," he said, uncertainly.

She waited.

"Maggie, do you still have that friend in the police department?"

"Enrico? Sure I do. I took his children out to Maryland a couple of weeks ago for the circus."

"Well," he said slowly, "do you think that Enrico could check on any dog licenses that might have been issued to the Semples? It's not important enough to lose any sleep over, but if he can do it easily . . ."

"I'll ask him. Incidentally, you ought to find some stray kids and use them as an excuse to visit that circus. It's coming to Washington in a couple of weeks, and it's really terrific. Do you like high wire acts?"

Gene managed a tired smile. "Sure I do. In this office, we don't do anything else."

While he was waiting for Maggie to dig out some background information on the Ubasti, he dialed Peter

Graves' number. An answering machine told him that Dr. Graves was engaged right now, but he could leave a message. He asked the psychiatrist to call him back. Then he paced around the office, fidgeting, and staring out of the window at a cold gray day with clouds that drifted across the sky like the ragged smoke from a distant battle.

One of the more curious aspects of last night's argument with Lorie was the mention of Smith's gazelle. It had cost Mathieu an enormous amount of physical effort to say it, and yet Gene couldn't see what the significance of it might be. He knew that it was an age-old method of catching and killing big game, this business of tying a kid or a sheep to a stake as bait, but he couldn't decide what the parallel was with his marriage to Lorie. Was Mathieu trying to warn him that Lorie was the bait for some design that her mother had on him? But what could her mother possibly hope to gain from having him marry Lorie? A little social distinction on the Washington cocktail circuit, perhaps, but hardly very much more. Maybe she had dreams that, one day, Gene would be Secretary of State.

Lorie herself had pointed to the etching of Smith's gazelle, as if it was some kind of explanation for everything that had happened. But whatever the explanation was, Gene couldn't work it out. His mind was direct and blunt, and he was usually baffled when it came to obscure metaphors and arcane puzzles.

He felt exhausted and disappointed, but he was also guilty that he had left Lorie so abruptly. He felt like calling her and telling her that everything was okay, but in the end he decided against it. The most important thing for him to do now was to make up his mind about her idiosyncratic body, and whether he was going to accept Lorie for what she was, or spend six weeks in Reno fixing himself a divorce. He wondered why the hell God had singled him out for a burden like this.

Maggie came back and found him asleep in his chair. She shook his shoulder gently, and he opened his eyes in shock.

"You've been dozing," she told him. "How do you feel?"

He blinked, and tried to stretch himself back into the real world.

"I was having nightmares," he said. "I keep having these nightmares about beasts and creatures, and they're all trying to chase me."

"Sounds like you're suffering from overwork and lack of sex," said Maggie.

Gene nodded, and pulled his lower eyelids down to wake himself up. "You're probably right," he said thickly. "All I need is a long vacation in a bawdy house."

She fixed him another cup of coffee, and then she sat down and opened a thin manilla file that she'd brought from records.

"Is that it?" he asked her. "It doesn't look like very much."

"That's because there isn't very much there. The librarian had never even heard of the Ubasti, and we only found any referance at all by accident. There's a book called *Wanderings in Lower Egypt* by a Victorian gentleman called Sir Keith Fordyce, and he mentions them briefly in passing, and there's also something about them in a topographical dispatch sent to Gordon at Khartoum, but that's all."

"What does Sir Keith have to say for himself?"

"I made a Xerox. It's all here."

She passed over a sheet of paper, and Gene read it

carefully through. It was one page from a closely printed Victorian book, and Maggie had also attached a copy of the steel engraving from the facing page. The picture showed a dark pile of stone ruins, under a forbidding sky, and the notes underneath said, "Tell Basta. All that remains of a magnificent ancient city, as seen from the Southeast."

The words from *Wanderings in Lower Egypt* read: "My guide had informed me in Cairo that many European opinions about the pyramids at Gizeh and about the sphinx were erroneous. He told me much that I already knew; that the word 'sphinx' itself was Greek for 'the strangler' and that the popular legend was that the sphinx was originally a monster with the head of a woman and the body of a lion. She, or it, would lie in wait for passers-by, and pose them a riddle. If they were able to answer it, she would let them go. If they were not, she would strangle them. But what I did not know was that among the fellaheen there are stories that the sphinx was copied from life, and that in the vastnesses of the southern desert there was a race of people who were actually descended from the carnal conjunction of women and lions. He became uneasy when he told me this, and he insisted that I pay him additional fees, because he said that even today the descendants of that dark and terrible people lived on, and guarded their obscene secret with a ferocious jealousy that had meant the murder of many a loose-tongued guide. Paid and given food, he went on to say that the lion-people had worshiped the cat-god Bast, a demonic being whose rituals had demanded human sacrifice, mutilation, and sexual perversities beyond the imagination of Christian minds. They lived in the city of Tell Basta, and even today no guide, including himself, could be persuaded to visit those ruins, for fear of retribution from what he could only describe as 'that people.' "

Gene laid the piece of paper down. He was shaking. He stared at Maggie as if she were a visitor from another world, and for a long while he was unable to speak.

"Gene, are you all right? Don't you think you'd better see a doctor? You look awful!"

He shook his head. His lips were dry, and there was a sour taste of cigarettes in his mouth.

" '*That people,*' " he whispered. "It's incredible."

"Gene, what's incredible?"

He passed the paper back to her, and pointed to the foot of the page. "It's all there," he told her. "It's crazy, and it's frightening, but it's all there."

She read it, but all she could do was shrug. "I don't see why it's crazy, and I don't see why it's frightening. It looks like a legend to me. I mean, isn't it?"

Gene went back to the window and watched the traffic. Finally, he spoke. "When I first went out with Lorie, she told me she belonged to a tribe of Egyptians called the Ubasti. Naturally, I didn't think anything of it. Why should I? I'd never heard of them. Then, later, she said that her tribe was always referred to by the Egyptian fellaheen as 'that people.' Apparently they were so terrifying, these Ubasti, that no one could bring themselves to speak their name out loud."

He came back from the window and straddled an office chair, looking Maggie straight and level in the eye.

"Last night, on our wedding night, when Lorie undressed—"

"Gene!" interrupted Maggie.

"Listen, will you?"

"But, Gene, that's private. I can't—"

"Will you please, for God's sake, listen! When Lorie

undressed last night, which she was very reluctant to do, I might tell you, she turned around and she had six breasts. And hair, brown curly hair, that came right up her stomach to here."

Maggie's mouth was open, and she was totally dumbstruck.

"Gene," she said, blinking, "are you putting me on?"

He swallowed. "It's the truth, Maggie. She has breasts here, like normal breasts, and then two smaller breasts underneath, and then underneath those, two nipples. She said . . . she said that American doctors call them 'supplementary breasts.' It's one of those . . . weird kind of conditions that happens now and again."

Maggie could only shake her head in agonized sympathy. "Oh, Gene, I'm so sorry. Oh, God, no wonder you're so upset. Listen, can't she have them removed by surgery? Or maybe hormone medication?"

"She won't," he said dully.

"She *won't*? What do you mean, she won't?"

"Precisely that. She thinks they're beautiful, and normal. And she's so convinced about it that, in the end, I decided to try and find out whether they *were* normal."

"How can they be normal? Six breasts? That's totally abnormal!"

Gene flicked the Xerox copy of Sir Keith Fordyce's book. "They might be totally abnormal for someone who had a human father and a human mother. But this book says the Ubasti were the descendants of '. . . a carnal conjunction of women and lions.' A girl who had the blood of lions flowing in her veins might have a few more lion-like characteristics, like rows of nipples to suckle her young, and excessive hair. And do you remember her eyes? Green, flecked with yellow. Like a lioness."

"Gene," said Maggie desperately, "you have to be making this up."

He lit a higarette. "Do you think I'd be sitting in the office on the day after my wedding if I was?"

She dumbly shook her head.

"Maggie, I appreciate everything you've done. I mean that. But I want to face up to this thing, and find out what it's really all about. Whatever Lorie's like, I married her, and I have a responsibility toward her."

"Have you ever thought she might be dangerous?"

"Dangerous? What do you mean?"

"Lions are dangerous, aren't they?"

"Yes, but——"

Maggie lowered her eyes. "I was thinking about what that French diplomat said."

"Which French diplomat?"

"The one who told you to 'beware of the dance.'"

"Well?"

"Well, I suddenly thought that he might have been speaking in French. You know how these diplomats slip into two or three different languages without even thinking about it. Perhaps he was telling you to beware of *les dents*."

"*Les dents*?"

"That's right. Beware of the teeth."

He found Peter Graves in the bar of the Arlington Golf Club. It was a dark, traditional place, with leather paneling and engraved pub mirrors, and there was a subdued babble of well-educated conversation, mingled with the occasional yelp of laughter. He ordered a straight Jack Daniels and scooped up a handful of cheese straws. It was lunchtime now and he hadn't eaten.

They shook hands. Gene was feeling tired and disinclined to talk to anyone, but he knew that he was going to have to make the effort before he went back to the Semple estate that night. He lit a cigarette. "Nice place you have here. All medical men?"

Peter shook his head. "Unh-hunh. Mostly military. A strategic bomb dropped on this place at lunchtime would wipe out most of the top brass at the Pentagon in a couple seconds."

"I'll remember that, next time I need to make a few bucks by selling secrets."

Peter was drinking whiskey sour. He dipped his cherry up and down in the froth, "How are you feeling?"

"Confused, mainly. Why?"

"You sounded pretty bad on the phone. I wondered for a moment if you were suffering from nervous hysteria."

"Hysteria? Me?"

Peter Graves finally put his cherry out of its misery and ate it. But he twiddled the stalk across to the ashtray and started poking the ash of Gene's ciragette with it.

"Hysteria happens even to the best-regulated minds. In fact, the best-regulated minds are more prone to it than those of us who are usually accused of 'woolly thinking.' There are five or six men in this bar alone—all top military men—who have suffered from acute hysteria. I've treated two of them myself."

"Successfully, I hope. I'm not sure I'm looking forward to World War Three."

"Who can say?" said Peter. "The kind of hysteria

I'm talking about can affect a man at a moment's notice."

"Well, that's very likely. But the truth is that I, personally, am not hysterical."

"You think you're married to a girl who's a cross between a human and a lion." Peter commented.

"I don't *think*, Peter, I *know*."

"How do you know? What proof do you have?"

"Jesus Christ, Peter, she has six breasts! I've seen them!"

Peter frowned. "I shouldn't shout things like that in here, Gene. They have a very conventional image of the world in here, and you might disturb their mental equilibrium."

"And what about you? It seems to me that you have a very conventional image of the world, too. You don't believe me, do you? You think I'm an interesting case, but right now you're trying to figure out what kind of syndrome can possibly induce a man to hallucinate extra breasts on his wife during their wedding night."

Peter sipped his drink. It left him with a white mustache.

"There are plenty of authenticated cases of supplementary breasts. I looked some up this morning. A woman in Baden-Baden had——"

"Peter, these are not supplementary breasts. She said herself that they ran in the family. They're an hereditary physical characteristic."

"You mean her mother has them as well?"

"I presume so, yes. That was the impression she gave me."

"We-e-ell," said Peter. "I must say that's pretty unusual."

Gene's drink arrived, and he took a hefty swallow.

The liquor burned down his throat and made him realize just how empty his stomach was.

"It's not unusual if you look at it the same way Lorie obviously does. She believes that her breasts are quite normal. Now, either she's suffering from some kind of psychological compensation for looking so odd, or else she's justifiably convinced that she's a real Ubasti woman and she's descended from these lion-people."

"Justifiably?" queried Peter. "You mean you believe they actually existed?"

"What else am I supposed to believe?"

Peter laced his fingers together and stared thoughtfully at the table. He was trying to do what all professional men are forced to do when someone confronts them with a completely unprecedented situation—fit it into a well-tried slot. Gene didn't think any the less of him for attempting to rationalize it, because he'd tried hard enough and long enough to rationalize it himself. But he knew that Lorie Semple Keiller, his bride of almost a day, had no rationale at all.

Peter absent-mindedly stroked his own bald head with his hand. "Do you love her?" he asked.

"Of course I love her. What makes you ask that?"

"Well," said Peter, "if you're going to help her, that's very important. If you don't love her, or if you're not sure that you do, then I suggest that you get yourself out of her life as quickly as you can. But if you do, and you really want to help her relate to the normal world, then you're going to have to buckle down to a couple of really tough decisions."

"You're going to suggest that I try and get used to them? The—the supplementary breasts? And the hair?"

Peter nodded. "You remember what I said at Walter Farlowe's party? If you're going to understand what it is with this girl, you're going to have to allow yourself to be carried along by what she thinks is her unavoidable destiny. From what you've told me, she has a fear that some event—some terrible and predestined happening—is going to come into both of your lives. What you have to do is play along with it all, and when it's plain to her that this awful event *isn't* going to happen, at that moment, you have your best chance to rehabilitate her."

Gene had a fleeting mental picture of Smith's gazelle. "And supposing it does happen?" he said. "Supposing, after all this, that she's right?"

Peter finished his drink. "Gene," he said blandly, "I want you to know one thing. I do not believe in the existence of lion-people. I'm sorry, but that's the way it is. It is genetically impossible for a lion to impregnate a woman, and even if it were possible, what would their descendants be doing in a nice house outside of Merriam, marrying nice young Democrats like you?"

Gene sighed. "All right, Peter. I know you find it hard to swallow. But I'm going back there, so whatever happens we'll probably find out the truth. I just hope that you're right and I'm wrong."

"As long as you love her, Gene, you've got a good chance of working it out."

Gene finished his Jack Daniels. "Just pray for me," he said quietly. "I think I'm going to need it."

She was waiting for him in the musty hallway, wearing a simple but very low-cut evening gown. Her hair was set in a cascade of shining curls, and she wore sparkling earrings and golden chains around her neck. Her décolletage was so deep that the pale pink areolas of her nipples showed, but as he hung up his raincoat on the hallstand and walked across the marble floor towards her, he made a conscious effort not to look. They were, after all, not the *only* nipples.

"Lorie," he said very softly, and then he leaned forward and kissed her. She closed her eyes, and he felt the tip of her tongue slip out from between her lips and into his mouth. It licked erotically at his teeth, and at his palate, but she still kept her mouth so closely sealed that he was unable to slide his own tongue back, and explore her teeth. Beware of *les dents,* said a cold voice at the back of his mind.

He stood back, and held both her wrists in his. She was smiling. A little unsurely, but plainly glad that he was here. "Gene, I missed you," and her eyes were glittering with tears.

At that moment, a deeper voice called, "Is that my errant son-in-law?" and Mrs. Semple, in an evening gown that was almost as revealing as Lorie's, came sweeping magnificently down the stairs. Her silver hair was freshly set and dyed, and she wore a necklace of pearls and silver.

"Mrs. Semple," said Gene, taking her hand. "I don't know what to say."

"You don't have to say anything, you wayward young man," said Mrs. Semple. "Lorie told me all about it, and I quite understand. Of course it was a shock! It was silly of Lorie not to warn you. But such things are so natural to us, to Lorie and me, that it didn't even enter her mind. Come on, dinner's ready in a few minutes, and I expect you'll want to change. You do look as if you've spent the day on a park bench."

A quarter of an hour later, they were seated in the dining room, while Mathieu, silent and formal in a badly fitting tuxedo, served them with bowls of hot clear consommé. This was one of the finest rooms in the house, with stained oak paneling imported from Europe, and a long polished Chippendale dining table that reflected the dipping and flickering light from the candles and the pale sunken moons of their own faces.

Lorie looked radiant as she sipped her wine, and she smiled across the table at him with such love that he found himself drawn back to her irresistibly. Whatever she was, whatever her origins were, she was unquestionably the most beautiful girl he had ever met, and perhaps that was all that mattered.

"Well, Gene," said Mrs. Semple, as she finished her soup. "Is there anything you want to talk about?"

"About today?"

"Of course."

"Isn't it kind of——"

Mrs. Semple raised her elegant hand, with its long curving fingernail. "In this family, Gene, we discuss everything, openly and freely. It is something that my dear late husband used to insist upon. He said there were enough secrets between enemies, without friends having secrets from each other, too."

"Well," said Gene uncomfortably, wiping his mouth, "it's a little difficult for me to explain. It was just that, well, physically, I wasn't prepared for Lorie at all. I mean, she isn't quite the same as most of the girls I've known."

"I see," replied Mrs. Semple, quite warmly and understandingly. "So you went away for a day to—how shall I put it?—reorient yourself?"

"In a manner of speaking."

"And are you now reoriented? Or are you still undecided?"

"I talked to that psychologist we met. You know, the one at Walter Farlowe's party? He said that if I truly loved you, Lorie, then I'd be able to accept you physically as you are. Well, he's a good man, and I guess I trust him. And I know, right above everything else, that I love you."

"Oh, Gene," whispered Lorie.

Mrs. Semple tinkled her bell for the next course.

"I'm very glad to hear you say that, Gene," she said, with a beam of satisfaction. "Now do try this fresh Canadian salmon. It's delicious."

He woke up during the night with a strange feeling that someone was muttering in his ear. He opened his eyes, and turned around, and he saw that Lorie was fast asleep, her tawny hair spread on the pillow, but that she was mumbling under her breath. He bent over to try and hear what she was saying, but it didn't seem to be words at all. Her breath was going in and out in a low, rumbling noise, as if she had some kind of congestion.

He checked his watch. It was two o'clock, and still impenetrably dark. He strained his eyes to look around the bedroom, but he couldn't see much. He lay back down again.

All of sudden, Lorie started to twitch, and shudder. Her breathing rasped in and out, and she tossed and flailed at the bedcovers, as if she were trying to fight something off. She snarled and snapped like a fierce animal, but at the same time she seem to be struggling with herself.

Gene switched on the bedside lamp. She still had her eyes tight shut and she was wrestling all over the bed, tugging at her long nightdress and clawing at the sheets. She was screaming and roaring in a harsh, low voice.

"Lorie!" he shouted. "Lorie—for Christ's sake!"

He tried to hold her arm, but she swung around with her other hand and clawed at his cheek with her nails.

He felt his skin scratched, and when he dabbed at his face with his sheet, it came away marked with blood. "You've scratched me!" he yelled.

Furious, frightened, he slapped her face so hard that he bruised his own hand. Lorie shuddered once more, and then lay still, her cheek inflamed from his slap, breathing in and out like someone running.

"Lorie," he hissed, "what the hell's going on? Lorie, talk to me!"

She lay there for a few more minutes, panting deeply and ignoring him, but then she slowly turned her head and stared at him. Her green eyes, with pupils tightly closed, looked menacing and cruel, and he remembered with a sensation of dread the merciless animal eyes that had watched him while he slept after his mauling by the dogs.

"Lorie?" he asked. "Lorie, is that you?"

Still staring at him, she gradually drew back her lips in a broad, vicious, naked snarl. Her teeth were yellow and curved and sharp. She lifted herself up on her hands, and began to crawl toward him across the bed. For a paralyzed moment, he thought he was going to find himself powerless to move, but as she crept closer he rolled off the side of the bed and stumbled halfway toward the bedroom door.

She crawled to the edge of the bed on all fours, and knelt there, her lips still drawn back in that leonine snarl, watching him and panting.

He felt chilled and prickled with fright. Whatever this beast was, it didn't seem to be Lorie at all. All of the evening's gentleness and radiance had drained out of her face, and she was glaring at him now with utter animal impassiveness. Her hair was ruffled now, like the mane of a lion, and the whole bedroom was pervaded by the musky scent of her body.

"Lorie," he whispered.

The beast's eyes opened wider and watched him.

"Lorie, if you're inside there, if you're inside that body . . . Lorie, listen!"

He edged back toward the door, picking up his bathrobe from the chair and wrapping it slowly around his right forearm. He had seen someone do that in a Tarzan movie when threatened by a lioness, and for some ridiculous reason it seemed like the best defense. But he didn't take his eyes off her, and she didn't take her eyes off him, and the tension between them—stalked and stalker, victim and intended prey—was unbearable.

"Lorie," he said huskily. "It's me! It's Gene! Don't you recognize me? It's Gene!"

What happened then had him stammering with terror. Lorie bounded down from the bed, on all fours, and leaped quickly towards the half-opened window. She pushed it wider with her hand, and then climbed up on to the narrow sill. She turned her head slowly around and regarded him with those green, closed, impenetrable eyes—and then before he could stop her, she jumped out of sight.

"Lorie!" he yelled.

He ran to the window and looked down. It was thirty feet down to the gravel, and she must have dropped like a stone. But in the shadowy darkness of the night, with the oaks rustling in a chilly October wind, there was nothing down there at all. No white nightdress sprawled on the drive. No broken Lorie. Nothing.

Out of the corner of his eye, he glimpsed a pale shape running toward the copse. It ran faster than almost anything he had ever seen, in long, loping strides.

Then it vanished in the darkness, and there was nothing at all but the creaking of the old house and the banging of a window that someone had left ajar.

Gene, trembling and numb, went across to the washbasin and drank a tumbler of water. Then he sat down on the bedside chair and lit himself a cigarette. His immediate response was to do something positive, like wake up Lorie's mother, or knock on Mathieu's door, or call the police, but he was beginning to understand that, with Lorie, he was going to need patience and subtlety.

Thinking about it now, a few minutes later, he could hardly believe Lorie's uncanny transformation. Maybe Peter Graves was right, and she was suffering from some kind of hysteria that made her believe she was a lion-person. But how did that account for a thirty-foot leap into the darkness—head first—with no apparent injury? And what about her scent, which still lingered?

It seemed from what he had witnessed tonight that there were two distinct sides to Lorie's personality. One side was gentle and caring, and unquestionably human. The other side was animal to the point of absolute cruelty. Yet he guessed that, somehow, these two personalities overlapped. When Lorie was in a state of complete humanity, she was obviously aware, from all the warnings she had given him, that she also had an animal side to her nature. And when, tonight, he had reminded the beast she had become that he was Gene, her husband, she seemed to be able to recognize him for what he was, and leave him safe.

There was something else that worried him, though. He went across to the bedside telephone and picked it up. He dialed Maggie's number, and waited for his persistent ringing to wake her.

After almost five minutes, she answered. She sounded terrible.

"Who the hell is this?" Do you know what time it is?"

"Maggie, it's me, Gene."

"Gene, for God's sake! It's two in the morning! I just got to sleep."

"Maggie, I'm sorry, but I have to ask you something."

Maggie sighed, but it was plain from the tone of his voice that he was alarmed and anxious, "Okay Gene, she finally said, "fire away." I just hope you haven't rung to ask my recipe for cinnamon cakes that's all."

"Maggie, it's the dogs."

"Dogs? What dogs?"

"You said you were going to ask Enrico to check on the Semples' dog licenses."

She sounded blurry. "That's right, I did."

"Well, what did he say?"

"He said they didn't have any dog licenses, and he even made sure by calling a buddy of his out at Merriam who knows the Semples pretty well. He doesn't think they have any dogs at all."

Gene took the phone away from his ear. Then that was it. On the night that he'd crept into the grounds of the Semple estate, looking for Lorie, he had probably found her. The beast which had dragged him down from the creeper and attacked him so viciously was his own wife.

"Thanks, Maggie. I'll probably call you tomorrow."

Then he went across to the window and closed it. He also went across to the bedroom door and turned the key. He dressed and lay down on top of the bedcovers to get some rest and await Lorie's return. Although he dozed, he didn't actually sleep, and horrifying images of Lorie's snarling face kept rising from out of the darkness.

Around dawn, when a grim washed-out light was just appearing at the window, he heard noises outside the door. He lifted his head from the pillow and listened hard. There were soft, scuffling sounds, like someone walking barefoot down the corridor. He rose as quietly as he could and tiptoed across the soft carpet to the door. He put his ear to it and strained to hear what was outside.

After a while, the door-handle slowly turned, and someone pushed firmly against the door. Realizing the door was locked, they rattled it, and pushed harder. Gene could feel the weight of a body against the pine paneling, and the hinges creaked.

There was another silence, and then the door was struck so hard from outside that it rattled.

More silence. Heavy, harsh breathing, and an odd sniffing sound.

Then a voice said, "Gene?"

He was sweating beads of icy perspiration, and he wiped his forehead with the back of his sleeve. It was Lorie, or the animal that Lorie had become. He found that his teeth were chattering, and he felt as if he was running a fever.

"Gene?" said the voice again, more coaxingly.

He kept his shoulder against the door, and his mouth tight shut.

"I know you're in there, Gene. Please open the door."

It sounded so much like the sweet, loving Lorie that he had married that he couldn't believe it. What the hell was he doing, keeping her locked out of their bedroom, when she was nothing more nor less than his own beautiful wife?

"Gene?" she whispered. "Open the door, Gene."

He said hoarsely. "I can't."

"Oh, please, Gene. It's cold out here. I'm cold."

"Lorie, I'm . . . I'm frightened."

A short silence.

"Frightened of me, Gene? Why?"

"Don't you know? Do I have to spell it out? How can I open this door when you might jump on me, the same way you did that night I climbed up the creeper?"

"Gene, you're not making sense."

He coughed. "Come on, Lorie, I'm making sense and you know it. As a matter of fact, I spent most of yesterday having my secretary look up the history of the Ubasti. I know what the Ubasti are now, Lorie, and I know why you look the way you do, and why you're proud of it."

"Gene," she said tenderly, "open the door. Let's talk."

"We're talking now."

"But it's cold out here, Gene. It's drafty. Let me in. I'm not going to harm you."

"How do I know? I might open this door and then you might leap on me."

"Gene—did you see the way I was? Did you see what I did, and how I couldn't even talk to you? Gene, I'm not like that now. Can't you hear that I'm just your wife?"

Gene bit his lip and stared thoughtfully at the key in the door. If he turned it, and let her in, he might be surrendering himself as weakly and easily as a Smith's gazelle. On the other hand, she might be right. Now that the animal phase seemed to have passed, she might be as harmless and affectionate as always.

"Wait a minute," he said. He stepped away from the door, and picked up a small wooden chair from the corner of the room. Then, keeping it raised in his right hand, he gingerly reached out with his left and turned the key.

"I've opened it," he called. "You can come in now. But, please, no sudden moves."

She didn't answer. Slowly, she turned the handle, and the latch clicked free. The door opened with a small shudder and swung gradually back on squeaking hinges.

He couldn't see her at first. Although it was dawn, the landing was still dark, and all he could make out was a tall, shadowy shape. He could hear her breathing, though, in low, purring gasps, and he could see the glint in her eyes.

"Okay, Lorie. Step inside."

She came forward two or three paces into the room. He backed off warily, holding the chair up like an amateur lion-tamer. When she reached the center of the room, next to the four-poster bed, she paused. It was still so gloomy that he found it hard to make her out.

"Lorie," he said. "Just stay there. I'm going to switch on the bedside lamp."

Reaching behind him, keeping his eyes on her motionless form, he groped for the switch. He found it, clasped it in the palm of his hand, and clicked it on.

He thought for a split second that she was dressed in a scarlet robe. But then, with almost intolerable disgust, he saw that she was naked, and that she was smothered in dripping blood. It clung in congealing grumes in her wild hair and surrounded her mouth as if she'd been guzzling at gory flesh. All down her front, all over her breasts, all down her thighs, the bright red liquid ran wet and glossy like a butcher's apron.

Six

"What have you done?" he whispered. Then shouted: "Lorie! What have you done?"

She pulled across to the washbasin, leaving bloody footprints on the carpet, and turned both faucets on full. Then she splashed her face and chest with water and wiped off the worst of the gore with a fasecloth and a towel.

"Lorie," said Gene, shaking, "Lorie, will you tell me what's happened?"

"I saved your life," she said quietly, looking away.

"You did what? Lorie, for Christ's sake——"

She turned and stared at him. "I saved your life by slaughtering a sheep. If I hadn't, then it might have been you."

He couldn't believe it. He was nearly hysterical. "You went out there tonight, with no clothes on, and you found a sheep and you killed it and ate it *raw*?"

She washed off some more of the blood. She seemed calm, but quite unrepentant.

"Does it surprise you?" she said. "You knew I was Ubasti. You knew that we are lion-people, my mother and I. Why is it any worse for us to kill and eat a sheep in the field than it is for you to eat a sheep that's been roasted and brought to the table?"

"But you said it might have been *me*! Supposing you hadn't saved my life? Supposing the lion instinct in you was too strong?"

She dried herself, and went to the wardrobe to choose a new nightdress. "It wasn't, and you were safe. That's all."

Gene felt a tide of nausea rising in his throat. He set down the chair he had been holding and reached in his pockets for a cigarette. There was only one left, and it was crumpled and bent. He straightened it and lit it.

"Lorie," he said, "you know that this is the end."

She was tying up the ribbons of a floor-length nightdress in yellow embroidered cotton. "You mean you're going to leave me?"

"I don't see what else I can do. I can't take any more of this. I can't trust you any more. How can I sleep with you, knowing that you might turn on me in the night and tear out my throat? It's not possible."

Lorie combed out her hair, then switched off the light over the washbasin mirror. She sat down on the edge of the bed, and looked up at Gene sadly and pensively.

"You must hate me," she said. "You must think I'm totally loathsome."

"Lorie," he said, "I don't think that. But I can't take this kind of situation any longer. It frightens the hell out of me. Don't you understand that?"

"Of course. I know what you must be feeling. But don't you see, Gene, that feeding like this is *natural* to me? To me, it's just as ordinary and uncomplicated as breathing."

He ran his hand through his hair. "Lorie, I can't take it! There is no way, no way at all, that I can take it. I mean, how often do you get like this? Is it every night? Or once a month? Or what?"

"I did hope, when we first got married, that you could help me," she said softly.

"Help you? What do you mean?"

"I hoped that it was possible to learn how to become nothing more extraordinary than your wife. Your ordinary, American wife. I hoped that you'd understand me, and that you'd teach me. This breed of Ubasti must come to an end somewhere, Gene. It has to die out sometime. I hoped that I was going to be the last."

"You mean, you and your mother, you're the last lion-people left?"

She nodded. "There may be others, but we've never seen or heard of them. The tribe was cast out of Tell Besta by the armies of the pharaohs long before Christ was born, long before Moses. They were spread all over the world, but very few of them survived. Many of them were killed or captured because they were more lion than human, and some of them simply found it impossible to adapt to human society. Our family, I suppose, was lucky. We were more human than beast, and we hid ourselves in Europe for hundreds of years. The lion strain only makes itself apparent through the women of the family, and so our name was always changing, and we were difficult to trace. Sometimes we invented names, like my mother's maiden name Masib. That's an anagram for Simba, the African word for lion."

"Your father . . . died, didn't he? Mauled to death. Was it really by bears?" Gene shuddered. "Or was it your mother?"

"Mother is very traditional," whispered Lorie. "She's not like me. She believes in all the old rituals."

"You mean she actually killed your father?"

"I don't know for certain. It is something that she never speaks about. But in the old books of Tell Besta, it is said that a lion-woman must always devour her mate after he has been of service to her."

"Of *service*?" queried Gene.

"It depends what she wanted her mate to do for her. I think that once my father had brought my mother to America, and set her up in the kind of lifestyle she wanted, and given her a daughter, then after that she had no further use for him."

Gene finished his cigarette, and ground it out in the bedside ashtray. He blew out smoke.

"And that was what was going to happen to me? Once I'd been of service and set you up in Washington society, you were going to rip me apart?"

"Gene," she said intensely, "you don't understand."

"Maybe I don't. Maybe I don't want to. Maybe all I want to do is get the hell out of this place. Lorie, can't you see what you're asking me to do? You come home naked and covered in blood, and you expect me to grin and say 'hi, dear, have a nice night?' "

"You said tonight that you loved me."

"Well this morning I'm not so sure."

"Gene, I thought you'd——"

"You thought I'd *what?*" he yelled. "You thought I'd sit back and allow myself to be treated like a dummy? Don't you understand what it took for me to come back here after I'd found out about your body? I loved you, and I thought that I could persuade you to have yourself changed. But as soon as I get back, you're out stalking your prey like some goddamned wild beast!"

"Gene, I want to change. I want to. You're my only hope."

"You didn't say you wanted to change yesterday. 'I'm Ubasti and proud of it,' that's what you said. 'Honoring and obeying doesn't include altering my racial characteristics.' Lorie, you're not even goddamned *human!*"

She flinched. For a moment, her eyes widened, but

then she seemed to relax, make a conscious effort to restrain the ferocious animal that ran inside her veins.

"Gene," she told him, "I love you."

He didn't answer.

"I'm your wife, Gene, whatever I'm like. I know you want me to change and I will. I'll go to the plastic surgeon, Gene, I mean it. I'll have these breasts removed. And I'll never go out again at night. I'll learn Gene, if you'll help me. Just help me, please. Even if you don't love me, even if you think I'm a revolting animal, please help me to shake off this terrible thing."

He coughed. "That's easy to say with a full belly, isn't it? What happens when you get hungry again? What happens when you feel like a mouthful of juicy red blood?"

"Gene, I promise."

"You don't have to. I'm leaving. My attorney will send you the divorce papers."

She went down on her knees on the carpet. She was crying.

"Get up," he snapped impatiently. "Crying won't help."

"Oh, Gene, just give me a chance. Please, Gene, please."

"I said *get up*!!"

At that moment, tall and forbidding in a long white robe, Mrs. Semple appeared at the bedroom door. Her hair was immaculately brushed and she was even wearing makeup. She came sweeping in, and she put her arms around Lorie's shoulders, staring up at Gene with a cold, distrustful glare.

"You've upset her," she said, accusingly. "Don't you know how sensitive she is?"

Gene gave an almost imperceptible nod. "I also

know how good she is at jumping out of second-floor windows and slaughtering sheep."

"She's a Ubasti, you fool!" hissed Mrs. Semple. "A living descendant of one of the proudest and rarest people on earth. Have you no understanding at all?"

"Oh, I understand all right. I've read all about the Ubasti."

"Then you'll know that you can't treat Lorie like a common housewife. Oh, Lorie, don't weep, *ma chère.* Look at her, Gene. Can't you see breeding and pride when you have it right in front of your nose?"

"What pride?" Gene said simply. "Pride as in 'pride of lions?'."

"Oh, Lorie," said her mother, "don't weep, darling, don't weep."

Gene went over to the dressing table and collected his cufflinks, his comb, and a few bits and pieces from his pockets. In the mirror he could see Mrs. Semple watching him, but he deliberately kept his back turned. He wanted to show her that he wasn't frightened, that he wasn't a helpless gazelle, even if his heart was bumping furiously and his hands were shaking.

"What are you going to do?" asked Mrs. Semple. "Are you going to leave this poor girl, desolate and abandoned?"

Gene didn't turn around.

"Are you going to let her struggle to survive on her own, a strange and rare creature in a world that hates her? Is that what you're going to do?"

"I'll see my attorney tomorrow," Gene said. "I'm sure we can work something out."

"You've decided, because she has fits of strange behavior, and because she has an appetite for fresh meat, that you don't love her any more? Just like that?"

"I didn't say that," Gene told her, in a hoarse voice.

"All I said was that I can't take this kind of behavior any more. I've already been bitten and badly injured once. Tonight I was threatened, and it was only sheer chance that I wasn't eaten alive. I can come to terms with some of the physical problems, and the whole thing about Lorie's ancestry, but I can't take the danger of it. Mrs. Semple, if you want to know the whole God's-honest truth, I'm scared shitless."

He went to the wardrobe to fetch his valise, and he packed away the few shirts that he had brought to the Semple mansion, along with his socks and ties. Lorie remained kneeling on the carpet, her hands covering her eyes, and her mother stayed beside her, gently stroking her daughter's hair.

"Well," said Gene, "I'm afraid that's it."

"You're sure?" said Mrs. Semple. "Even if I give you guarantees?"

"Guarantees? What guarantees?"

"Well," said Mrs. Semple, "supposing I guarantee your safety, and your peace of mind."

"How can you do that?"

"At night, we could lock Lorie in the next room, the small room where you stayed before. You could have the key. Also, Mathieu could lend you his rifle. You could keep it beside the bed, and if you were ever in any danger from anyone, you would be very well protected."

"Is that what love's turned out to be? A locked door and a loaded gun?"

Mrs. Semple stood up, and took his hand. "Gene, it won't last for long. Once she knows that you're going to stay with her, and that you're going to help her forget that she's a Ubasti, she'll slowly get better. Gene, you love her. You can also rehabilitate her. Make it possible for Lorie to live like a normal human being.

Can't you see how damned she is without your love? She will never love another man as much as you. Do you want her to stay like this for the rest of her life?"

"Supposing she comes in to attack me one night? Supposing I'm put in the position of having to shoot her? Then what?"

"It won't happen. The gun is simply for your own peace of mind."

"How can you be sure? What about your own late husband? Is that what happened to him?"

"He died in Canada, Gene. He was mauled by a bear."

"You mean it *looked* as if he'd been mauled by a bear."

Mrs. Semple released his hand and went back to Lorie, who was now sitting on the edge of the bed, cradling herself in her arms as if she was cold.

"I know what your suspicions are, Gene, and I know you've had a bad shock. I can only ask you to forgive us."

Gene licked his lips. He felt uncertain now. Walking out on Lorie would certainly be the safest and easiest thing to do, but how much of a man would he be if he did that? How much of a husband? He knew that she could possibly be dangerous, but she had never done anything worse than a woman who was spasmodically psychotic. Perhaps with some help from Peter Graves, the psychiatrist, he could actually train Lorie to become completely human. After all, real lions and tigers had been successfully trained to be docile. Why couldn't a creature that was already halfway human do the same?

"Please, Gene, don't leave me," Lorie said, the melting sound of her words finally convincing him.

"Okay," he said heavily. "We'll give it one more try.

But this time, we do it my way. We arrange the plastic surgery. We go to see a qualified psychiatrist. And we make sure that the bedroom door stays locked and bolted until I decide that I'm good and ready to let you out."

He went across to the bed and he held Lorie in his arms. Next to them, with a feline smile, Mrs. Semple was almost purring with satisfaction.

Peter Graves came out of his consulting room and closed the door behind him. He looked deeply thoughtful. Gene, who had been sitting reading tattered copies of *Time* magazine, looked up. "Well? What do you think?"

Peter sat down, and rested his chin in his hands. "She's a strange one, all right," he said, uninformatively. "In fact, she's one of the strangest ones I've ever seen."

Gene laid down his magazine. "Listen, Peter, I know that already. That's why we're here. What I want to know is, what's wrong, and what can you do about it?"

Peter sat back. "Well," he said slowly, "it's not one of those psychoses that you can cure by driving at it with a bulldozer. In fact, I'm not so sure it's a psychosis at all."

"If it's not a psychotic condition, what is it?"

"I'm not too sure. You see, in layman's language, a psychosis is a disturbance of the personality in which the subject's relation to reality is seriously impaired, but in this case, you wife seems to have a very consistent view of reality, even though the reality she's talking about is somewhat . . . unusual."

"You mean she's not disturbed?"

"I wouldn't say so, no. You can seek a second opinion if you like. She's slightly neurotic about her relationship with you, and she feels guilt because she told you some lies, but otherwise she seems as sane as anyone else."

"What about this unusual reality?"

Peter shrugged. "It's unusual because, unlike you or I, she thinks it's perfectly normal to have more than one pair of breasts, and to slaughter animals and eat their meat raw. But there's no suggestion that this attitude is brought about by a psychotic illness. Whatever the physiological makeup of her mentality may be, her brain cells appear to regard such things with complete equilibrium and dispassion. Her EEG reading was undisturbed and regular, and the only times when she became anxious was when we talked about you, and how you felt about her. She's very concerned about pleasing you, you know."

"Do you really think she's a lion-woman?"

Peter pulled a face. "Who knows? She certainly has some sexual characteristics that resemble a lioness, and there is some ingredient in her mental makeup that makes her behave in a related manner, but that's about as far as it goes."

"Peter—I saw her leap from a second-floor window, hands first, like a cat, and she wasn't even hurt."

Peter frowned. "Are you sure you wouldn't like a little course of analysis yourself?"

"Peter, I swear it."

"Well," said Peter, "I just don't know. I've never come across anything like it I've looked up a couple of cases where people have had freakish bodies, and have required psychoanalysis, but in most of these cases the subjects are worried about the way they look and, despite their outward appearance, are inwardly normal. What strikes me about your wife is that she is so utterly consistent about herself. There isn't a flaw in her personality anywhere."

"So what can I do? What happens if she turns nasty?"

Peter sighed. "I think the only option open to you is to go on treating her with love and affection, and try to show her what you want from her in terms of daily behavior. If she starts acting ferocious, tell her you disapprove. Gradually, the incentive to play out this lion-woman role will become less and less attractive to her."

"What about this predestined future of hers? Did she tell you anything about that?"

"No, she didn't. But she still thinks it's going to happen."

Gene scratched the back of his neck. "Any clues what it might be? Or when?"

"None at all. I'm sorry. She just said that 'Bast demands it,' whoever Bast might be. Someone you know?"

Gene stood up, feeling tired and depressed. "Yes," he said quietly. "Someone I know."

For the next three weeks, they continued to live at the Semple mansion in a strange ritualistic existence that seemed to take them farther and farther away from any kind of reality, Gene's or Lorie's. They had all agreed that Merriam was more secluded than Gene's apartment in Washington, and that until they were satisfied with Lorie's progress toward normalcy, they ought to stay away from the city at night. Gene still arrived for work every morning on Pennsylvania Avenue, but Maggie and even Walter Farlowe noticed that he was increasingly withdrawn, and there were dark circles under his eyes, as if he never slept properly. The truth was that he never did. Every night,

Gene locked his bride of less than a month into the small bedroom next to his, and then locked his own door before stretching himself out on the zebra-skin, four-poster. He kept the key to Lorie's door around his neck on a chain, and alongside his bed, never far from his sleeping hand, lay a 30–30 big game rifle that had been silently given to him by Mathieu.

Lorie still went to work at the Franco-African Bank, and quite often they met during the day for lunch or coffee. She seemed more composed these days, although she was sometimes inexplicably distant and remote and seemed to have her mind on something far away and long ago. Gene frequently had to repeat himself several times before she answered his questions.

In the evening, if they weren't attending a Washington party or if Gene wasn't working too late, the ritual was always the same. They dined by candlelight, with Mrs. Semple usually dominating the conversation with her memoirs of Egypt and the Soudan, and then they listened to music or watched television and eventually retired to bed. Gene kissed Lorie goodnight at her bedroom door, then closed it and turned the key. He always tested it to make sure it was locked properly. He always called, "Goodnight, Lorie. Sleep well," through the door. And he always listened for an answer, even though an answer never came.

Later, he would lie in bed, staring sleeplessly at the canopy above him, and wonder if he could hear her breathing, or scratching at the door. In the morning, around seven, he would rise from his hours of uncomfortable dozing, and go to release her from her noctunral prison. She was always smiling, always beautiful, always gentle, and as the days went by and the memory of his first horrific nights with her began to fade away, the reality of locking her up became increasingly hard for him to support. Only a nervous instinct deep inside him kept him true to his nightly charade; that, and the etching of Smith's gazelle.

Lorie never mentioned her imprisonment and appeared to accept it as calmly and rationally as she had accepted the fact of her own lion-like body. But this very calmness made it more difficult for Gene to communicate with her. He began to think that she would stay like this for ever, content to live a curious half-life as someone who was not completely animal and not completely human.

She was booked into the private clinic of the plastic surgeon, Dr. E. Beidermeyer; and, again, she appeared to take the idea of forthcoming surgery placidly and quietly. Whenever Gene tried to talk about it, and reassure her that everything would be fine, she would simply smile and say "I know," as if she was aware of something in the air that was going to change everything. Mrs. Semple, too, seemed to share Lorie's unknown secret, and by the end of the third week, Gene felt that he was the only man on a sinking ship who didn't know that the hull had sprung a leak.

One Thursday night, as he took her up to her bedroom for the usual locking-up, he said, "Some day soon, you're going to forget what Ubasti ever meant. I can feel it."

"Do you think I will?"

"You will if you want to. Do you really want to?"

She looked across at him with a slightly regretful expression. Behind her, the light from the stained-glass window seeped dimly down the wide staircase.

"Sometimes I don't know."

He pushed open the bedroom door for her. "If you want to stay the way you are, I'm not going to force you, Lorie. But I can't remain your husband if you do."

She smiled at him wanly. "Maybe we ought to take the next step now," she said. "Maybe it could help me change my mind."

"What next step?"

"Maybe you ought to invite me into your bedroom. It's what husbands and wives do, you know."

He said nothing.

"Gene," she told him, touching his arm, "we can't get any place if we carry on like this. I don't mind it, I don't mind you locking me in. I know how you feel. But our marriage isn't even a marriage yet, not properly, and how can we ever make it one if we don't try?"

He turned away, embarrassed.

"You loved me enough to stay with me, and try to make it work," she said. "Couldn't you show me how you love me with your body?"

He looked back at her, and tried to read what she was thinking in her eyes. They were as green and impenetrable as always.

"If I let you in," he said hoarsely, "I have no guarantees that you won't——"

"No," she said, "you haven't."

He looked down at the key in his hand. Did it really mean the difference between survival and death, or was he going through this whole absurd business to satisfy his own exaggerated neuroses? After all, Lorie hadn't tried to kill him before, when they were sharing the four-poster bed. All she'd done was go out and slaughter a sheep. And, as she'd pointed out herself, what made roasting that sheep and serving it up on a plate any more moral than eating it raw?

He was still standing there, undecided and hesitant,

when Mathieu came trudging up the stairs, stony-faced and silent. He saw them in the corridor, and paused.

"Goodnight, Mathieu," Lorie said, in a way that was an obvious dismissal. But Mathieu stayed where he was, his scarred hand on the banistair rail, and made no attempt to go.

"Well, Gene," said Lorie, with a quick smile, "perhaps some other night."

Gene looked at her questioningly, and then at Mathieu. Whatever silent communion had taken place between them, it had persuaded Lorie pretty promptly to change her mind about visiting his bedroom. She kissed him a fleeting goodnight, and then went inside and closed her own door. Mathieu watched as Gene put the key in the lock and turned it. Then, apparently satisfied, he continued on his way down the landing.

"Mathieu," called Gene. The mute stopped, his broad back as impassive as his face.

"Mathieu, is something going to happen here? Something I don't know about?"

Mathieu didn't move. Gene couldn't be sure if he was taking his time in answering, or waiting to be asked something else.

He walked around and faced the chauffeur, looking as intently as he could into those blank, suspicious eyes.

"You warned me once, didn't you?" he asked him. "When you mentioned Smith's gazelle, that was a warning. But that isn't everything, is it? There's something more. There's something more to do with Bast."

"Bast?" croaked the mute, squeezing the word from his larynx. Then he shook his head. But he reached out and held Gene's wrist, and said, in the same ghostly whisper, "Sons of Bast . . . sons . . ."

"Sons of Bast? What do you mean?"

Mathieu tried to breathe out some words, but his vocal strength was gone. Instead, in a grotesque attempt to explain, he dragged back his face with his hands into a hideous mask, and bared his teeth. Gene recoiled, and said, "That's the sons of Bast? That's what they look like?"

Mathieu nodded. He was about to try and explain further, when they heard the clicking of heels on the wooden staircase. It was Mrs. Semple, coming up to bed. Mathieu waved his hands as if he were wiping the images of his dumb-show out of the air, and went quickly off into the darkness.

Gene was still standing there when Mrs. Semple appeared.

"Hello, Gene," she said, in her contralto voice. "Is Lorie in bed now?"

He nodded. "Tucked in and locked up."

She came over and laid her hand sympathetically on his shoulder. He smelled that musky aroma of hers, and he could even feel her sharp fingernails through his shirt. Her eyes twinkled just like her circular diamond earrings.

"You mustn't worry, you know," she purred. "Quite soon, everything will be wonderful. You'd be surprised how much a Ubasti woman respects her mate."

He ran his hand tiredly through his hair. "Well, I hope so, Mrs. Semple. To tell you the truth, I don't know how much more of this I can stand."

"You love her, don't you? And you know that she loves you?"

"Sure."

"Well, let that be your guiding light, Gene. Let that inspire you in those dark moments when you doubt yourself."

He looked at her hard. He couldn't quite make up

his mind whether she was speaking sincerely or not. But her face was as passive and serious, and he decided that she must be.

"All right, Mrs. Semple," he said softly. "I'll try."

The next morning *The Washington Post* carried a small story at the foot of the front page whose headline read: "Dead Boy Attacked by Tigers?" Gene picked it up off his desk and read through it quickly. "Police suspect that nine-year-old Andrew Kahn, whose mutilated corpse was discovered yesterday by drainage workmen, was attacked and killed by a large, predatory beast, like a tiger. Their theory, which they admit is 'a trifle difficult to credit,' has come after an intensive autopsy on young Andrew's body. Although full details are being withheld, it is understood that he was almost unrecognizable when found, and that much of his body was missing, as if consumed or strewn about by a wild animal. There are no reports of any creatures of the size of a tiger missing from any public or private menageries."

Gene laid the paper down. Then, his face white, he went to the men's room, and vomited his breakfast into the basin.

Dinner that evening was tense and solemn. Mathieu brought bowls of steak soup, and the three of them sat in the flickering light of the candles, their eyes watchful and alert. Lorie was wearing her low-cut gown again but her mother was dressed in a formal high-necked dress with a cameo pinned to the collar.

Sipping her soup, Mrs. Semple said, "We're all a little quiet tonight."

Lorie gave an uneasy grin. "It's Gene. He's been lost

in some dark reverie of his own ever since he got back home. Haven't you, Gene?"

"What?"

"There you are," said Lorie. "You haven't even been listening!"

"I'm sorry," Gene apologized. "I was someplace else."

"Anywhere interesting?" asked Mrs. Semple, raising a beautifully plucked eyebrow.

Gene laid down his spoon. "It depends where you consider interesting. As a matter of fact, I find abandoned drains just outside of Merriam pretty interesting."

Lorie glanced at her mother. Mrs. Semple said: "Abandoned drains? Whatever are you talking about?"

"I guess you could say that I'm being hysterical. It's not so difficult when you're tired, and under a constant strain. But the whole thing seemed too much of a coincidence, you know? A round peg fitted neatly into a round hole."

"Gene, dear, I do think you've been overworking," Mrs. Semple said.

"Have I?" retorted Gene. "Or is it you, and my newlywed wife? Maybe *you've* been overworking?"

"I really don't know what you're talking about," said Lorie, hotly. "You've been in a terrible mood all evening, and now you're talking in ridiculous riddles. Why don't you make sense?"

"You didn't see the paper this morning?" asked Gene.

"Why should I?"

"You didn't see the television, either?"

"Well, no, as a matter of fact, I didn't."

Gene pushed away his plate of soup and stood up. He walked around the table until he was standing just behind Mrs. Semple, so that if she wanted to look at him she had to twist uncomfortably around in her chair.

"In the paper this morning they reported that the body of a nine-year-old boy had been found in a drain near Merriam. The police said that he looked as if he'd been eaten by wild animals. Tigers, they said. Something of that size."

Lorie frowned. "Gene," she said, "You're not suggesting that——"

"What else am I suppose to suggest? What other conclusion can I possibly come to?"

"Are you trying to tell me that Lorie killed a child? Is that it?" Mrs. Semple said.

"I'm not telling you. I'm asking you. The facts are there in the paper, and I'm asking you."

"And supposing she says no?"

"Then I guess I'll have to believe her. But I won't find it easy."

"So you really think she could have done it?" asked Mrs. Semple.

"I don't know. Perhaps she ought to tell me for herself."

Mrs. Semple stood up, too.

"If the answer is not no, if the answer is yes, then what did you propose to do about it?"

"I think that's one of those bridges we'll have to cross when we come to it."

"Gene," said Mrs. Semple, in that vibrant contralto of hers, "you must remember that Lorie is your wife. You owe her your love, and your trust. You can't treat her like a criminal. We've all agreed to give in to your little whims, and let you lock her in her room at night, but if we're going to have to put up with hysterical accusations every time there's an item in the newspaper that sounds as though there were lions, or tigers, or any other kind of wild beast involved, then all I can say is that you had better think again about your marriage, and perhaps decide to end it."

"Mrs. Semple, you know I don't want to do that," Gene retorted. "Not until we've seen how Lorie makes out. Maybe, after the plastic surgery——"

Mrs. Semple sniffed disdainfully. "You're such an American! All that matters to you is outward appearances! As long as Lorie *looks* like the kind of girl you want to be married to, then everything is perfect. But while she still has the body of a Ubasti, you persecute her, just as every Ubasti has been persecuted for thousands of years. And now you come out with this preposterous story about a boy who was killed by tigers. Does it make sense? Really?"

"Gene, you must learn to trust me. Please." Lorie said.

Gene looked at Mrs. Semple, and then at Lorie. He lowered his eyes, and said in a hoarse and stubborn whisper, "I don't know what to believe any more, Lorie, and I don't know who to trust. I think the best thing I can do right now is leave. Then you won't have the burden of my suspicions any longer, and you won't have to put up with my neurotic behavior. You can live your life the way you want to, whether you want to live like a lion or live like a human being. I've tried to help you Lorie, and I can't. It's beyond my capabilities."

Lorie laid down her napkin, pushed back her chair, and came around the table. She held out her hands for Gene, and her face was, so loving and sympathetic that he could hardly look at her.

"Gene," she said softly, "don't you realize how much I love you? How much I need you?"

He didn't answer.

"Don't you realize that the moment I first saw you at Henry Ness's party I knew you were perfect, that you were just what I'd always been looking for?"

"Lorie," he said tiredly, "the strain is just getting too much for me. I know you love me, and I know that you need me. But I'm not sure I can carry that load any longer. Not when my trust in you is constantly being put to the test."

"Do you want to believe that Lorie killed that boy?" Mrs. Semple asked.

Gene went to the table and poured himself a glass a wine. "No, I don't," he replied, in a husky voice. "It's the last thing in the world I want to believe."

"Then don't," Mrs. Semple said. "It's as simple as that."

Gene drank almost the entire glass of wine in three gulps, and wiped his mouth with the back of his hand. "Lorie," he said, "I'd like to hear that from you."

"Hear what, Gene?"

"That you didn't kill him. That you went out that night and killed a sheep, nothing but a dumb sheep."

Lorie reached out and began to stroke the side of Gene's brushed-back hair, staring almost absent-mindedly into a distance that he could only guess at. Even though Gene felt so demoralized and exhausted, he couldn't deny that she was still warm and sensual and extravagantly beautiful, and there was something about her that still stirred him. Maybe he was drawn toward her by the very fright which she aroused in him, maybe he was transfixed, like a snowshoe rabbit, by the hypnotic glare of a lynx. Or maybe he did, after all, really love her and want their marriage to work in spite of every hazard and terror it held for him.

"You really think that newspaper story could be true?" asked Lorie simply.

He reached up and held her wrist. "Why don't you tell me it's not true instead of asking me? Why don't you just come straight out and tell me?"

"Because you have to trust me," said Lorie. "You have to trust my love for you or it's no good at all. Even if I had killed someone, would that make you stop trusting my love?"

"Well, I don't know. I guess not."

"Then what does it matter whether I killed that boy or not?"

Gene splashed himself another glass of wine. "Lorie, I don't know what to say. I don't know what to tell you. I can't deny that I still feel, I don't know, you can call it whatever you like. Suspicious, mistrustful, frightened. Cowardly. I just don't know where to go from here."

"Gene," Mrs. Semple said, "you and Lorie are at the crossroads now. You can go further, and explore your love, and overcome all your fears. Or you can continue to treat Lori with suspicion and alarm, and not get anywhere at all. You have to believe her, Gene, and how can you believe in her if every mention of wild animals in the newspapers is going to strain your relationship to the breaking point? How can you make a marriage work if every night there is a locked door between you, even after that locked door is no longer necessary?"

"Mrs. Semple, I hate to remind you, but you suggested the locked door in the first place."

"Of course I did. But it wasn't to keep Lorie imprisoned. I trust her. The door was locked to make *you* feel more sucure, so that you would stay and get to know Lorie better."

There was a long, difficult silence. Then Gene said,

"Mrs. Semple, are you saying that Lorie doesn't need to be locked in? That if I ask her, she won't go out nights any more?"

Mrs. Semple nodded. "It's all a question of trust."

"But before, that night when she went out, she said she'd had to kill that sheep to save my life, so that she'd wouldn't be tempted to tear me to shreds."

"Gene, just as you are adapting to Lorie, Lorie is adapting to you. And anyway, things have changed."

"What do you mean, changed?"

Mrs. Semple looked at him with her green, lambent eyes. "Stay for one more week. Give Lorie seven more days. Then you'll discover just how much things have changed."

Gene turned to Lorie. "Are you trying to tell me you've lost you appetite for raw flesh? You don't need fresh blood any more? Is that it? Are you really adapting that much?"

"Trust me, Gene," Lorie said. "I beg you."

Gene attempted a grin. He was feeling as fragmented and unreal as a smashed mirror. "How about that?" He said uneasily. "I come home full of terrible accusations, and we end up closer than ever."

"The Ubasti are used to terrible accusations, Gene," Mrs. Semple said. "They are also among the fiercest and strongest lovers that the world has ever known. Perhaps love is nourished by persecution."

Gene paused, his eyes on the table. He knew that he didn't have to stay. But if he didn't, what was he going to do? He had invested so much effort and stamina into making their relationship work that leaving it now was just as grisly a prospect as carrying on. If it *did* work, if they *did* make it together, what a rare and fantastic couple they could be! He could think of her now, making her entrance at Washington society parties on his arm, in her low-cut gown and her glittering diamonds. That's Gene Keiller, the up-and-coming young State Department executive, and that's the gorgeous and mysterious lion-lady he managed to tame.

In the polished wax of the table, his own face peered blearily up at him. He took a deep breath.

"All right, Mrs. Semple," he said. "I'll stay, at least for a week."

Lorie smiled, with obvious relief and said, "Thank you, Gene. I won't let you down."

He took her hand, and gently squeezed it. "I guess you're right about trust. I've got to learn to believe in you."

"Don't rush it," said Mrs. Semple. "Keep Lorie's door locked as long as you want. The night that you leave it open, then we'll know that you've come to us trustingly, and that you really want to be a member of the family."

Gene lit a cigarette, and didn't see the quick, intensive glance that passed between mother and daughter. Nor did he see Mathieu standing silently at the door, watching them all through a half-inch crack with his usual stony face.

He was exhausted that night, and they went to bed early. On the landing he gave Lorie a parting kiss before locking the door, and stood there holding her hand for a few moments, trying to shape the words in his mind that would tell her he still loved her, that she still turned him on, but that someplace deep at the back of his mind was the instinctive fear that once he relaxed his guard, something would go wrong and she would attack him.

"You must think I'm the most suspicious bastard on God's earth," he told her.

She shook her head. "I don't think that."

"Well, I would if I were you. I don't know how you've stood this relationship so long."

"I've told you, Gene. I need you."

He leaned back against the oak paneling of the corridor and rubbed his eyes. "Terrific husband I turned out to be."

She put her arm around his shoulder and kissed him. Then she held him very close, staring into his eyes.

"You've been wonderful, Gene. Most men would have left by now."

"I still don't . . . trust you, though, do I?"

"You will."

He kissed her back. She still kept her lips closed, but her lips were soft and moist enough to arouse him.

"That change your mother was talking about. Do you know what she means?"

Lorrie nodded.

"And you can't tell me what it is?"

"Not yet. The time isn't right yet."

"Soon."

She nodded again. "Very soon, darling. Sooner than you think."

He fell asleep quickly, and dreamed of lions and tigers and ferocious jaws that snapped at his heels. He was desperately trying to run away from a huge beast that loped after him, tearing at his legs and his ankles. Then he was being smothered by a suffocating pelt of fur, and he was choking. He woke up, sweating and shaking, and it was still only two in the morning.

He sat up in bed. The bedroom was very dark. The window was open and a rainy wind was making it shudder and rattle. He climbed out of bed and padded on bare feet across to the basin to pour himself a glass of water.

Outside somewhere, he thought he could hear a door or window banging. When he'd gulped down the water, and dabbed his mouth on a towel, he walked across to the window and put his head out, to see if he could see where it was.

The night was stormy black and the trees around the house champed like ghostly horses. Leaves were tossed over the old rooftops of the Semple mansion, and the chimneys howled and moaned in vibrant complaint at the wind.

In the darkness, Gene was sure that he could see something pale and large moving on the wall that came out from beside his bedroom at right angles. He squinted into the rain and the wind, trying to make out what it was. The shape was at least thirty or forty feet up the wall, on a narrow ledge that couldn't have been more than six inches wide. One minute he could see it moving in a pattern of the shadows, and the next it was gone altogether. He stayed at the window for three or four minutes, but the rain was getting heavier, and he didn't see anything else.

He closed the window and turned back into the room. In the darkness, there was a disturbed frown on his face. Supposing, just supposing, that shape had been Lorie? Supposing she had betrayed his trust, had gone out at night again, on the prowl for fresh blood?

He could go check her room. But how much would that betray *his* trust? If he was ever going to believe her, he would have to accept her word.

For half an hour, while the rain lashed against the windows of his room, he paced up and down, trying to persuade himself that he had enough faith in Lorie not to go next door. But all the time he knew that he had to know for sure. If she was going to take on the menacing form of a lioness, and go out nights, he had to know.

He picked up the 30–30 big-game rifle from beside the bed, and clicked a round into the chamber. Then, wrapped in his bathrobe, he quietly opened the door of his room, and peered out into the dark corridor. The old house creaked in the wind, and that window was still banging somewhere, banging and banging with no one to close it.

He stepped out into the corridor, holding the rifle under his arm. Softly, he trod the two or three paces to Lorie's door. He stood there hesitantly for a moment, but he couldn't back down now. He lifted the key that hung round his neck on a chain, and with infinite care and quietness, he inserted it into the lock.

The lock levers clicked and he waited, holding his breath to hear if there was any sound from within Lorie's room.

He put his left hand on the doorknob, and turned it. Then he slowly pushed the door inward, and strained his eyes to distinguish her bed, and *her*, if she was there, in the gloom.

It was too dark to distinguish anything. He waited a little longer, and then he stepped stealthily into the bedroom, his rifle raised and one hand out in front of him to prevent him from bumping into any chairs or tables.

He circled the end of Lorie's bed, and came up close to the pillow. He leaned forward, and she was there all right, with her tawny hair spread out on the linen, and her eyes closed. She was breathing regularly and deeply, and her hand was raised to her parted lips as innocently as a sleeping child.

Carefully, cautiously, he backtracked out of the

room, closed the door behind him, and relocked it. He stood in the corridor for a while, listening to the noises of the house, and then he went back to his bedroom.

The shape he had seen on the wall was probably nothing more than the shadow of a tree, waving in the wind. After all, nothing human could perch on a six-inch ledge forty feet above the ground and disappear with such grace and ease. And if Lorie was safely asleep in her bed . . .

Gene felt a little ashamed, but he was also glad that he'd checked. From now on, he knew that he could begin to trust Lorie and build up something between them that wasn't strained by fear and mistrust. He still felt concern about that night she had come back smothered in blood, but he told himself that any aberration could be overcome, any psychosis calmed, and that if he gave his trust to Lorie with enough conviction, he could lead her out of the fierce and unnatural life she had been living up until now, and into peace and sanity.

He was so relaxed when he returned to bed that he drifted off into sleep almost at once and didn't hear the shuffling and bumping that disturbed the house an hour or so later. It sounded like something being dragged upstairs, step by step, like a sack, or mattress, or a dying boy.

Seven

That week was memorable in Washington for two reasons. The first was a man arrested for trying to run across the White House lawns with what appeared to be a gun, but was later discovered to be a piece of Kentucky fried chicken. He had told the police, "I just wanted to share my lunch with the President. He said he wanted to be a people's President didn't he?"

The second was the annual visit from the Romero Traveling Circus, which came a week early because of a cancelation at Silver Spring, Maryland.

It was still strangely warm for the time of year, and when Gene drove down the freeway on his way to work he kept the driving window of his car open. The big top was pitched out by the cloverleaf not far from the Merriam turnoff, and Gene could see the flags and the sideshows and the animal cages, and catch a waft of that distinctive smell of sawdust and cotton-candy and lions' urine.

At the office, Maggie knew that something had subtly altered in Gene's relationship to Lorie, and she tried to be more sympathetic and supportive. She had gone back home and cried the night that Gene had married Lorie, but now she saw herself as a friend and advisor to help him through the hard times of rehabilitating Lorie to live a completely human existence. She was always there when he was anxious or disturbed, and she could sense his moods and worries as soon as he walked into the office door.

Today, he seemed in pretty good humor.

"Are you going to see the circus?" she asked, collecting his completed reports from his OUT-tray.

"Who needs to see a circus when they work for Henry Ness?" asked Gene.

"It's a terrific show. You ought to go. Take Lorie."

Gene lit his first cigarette of the morning. "I can't say that I've ever liked circuses. I didn't even like them when I was a kid. All those elephants holding on to each other's tails. It's like a Democratic convention."

Maggie laughed. "Do you want some coffee?"

"I'd prefer some help."

"Help? What help do you want? You look like you've got everything pretty well sewn up these days."

Gene leaned back in his chair. "Well, things are a lot happier with Lorie. I mean, we're really beginning to relate to each other now. We're starting to build up our trust. With any luck, once she's undergone that plastic surgery, we'll be over the worst of it."

"But what?"

"I didn't say 'but' anything."

"Yes, but the 'but' was implied. You're happier with Lorie, you're looking forward to the plastic surgery, you're settling down in Dracula Castle, *but*."

Gene grinned. "If I'd have married *you*, I wouldn't have gotten away with anything. All right, I'll tell you what it is. It's this whole Ubasti thing, right? It's obviously very important to Lorie, and even more important to her mother, but they won't talk about it. It's like a secret between them, and I'm not included. I get some vague hints about the lion-people now and again, but that's not enough. Yet I think if I *knew* something about the Ubasti, what they really are, I might be able to relate to Lorie a lot closer."

Maggie shrugged. "I think you'd be doing yourself a favor if you let well enough alone for now. If Lorie doesn't want to tell you, then maybe she finds it too traumatic. You're going to have to build up your relationship absolutely firm before you can start poking around with the real sensitive stuff."

Gene stood up and stretched. "I don't know. I just get the feeling that everybody in the household knows something that I don't. It's like the chauffeur, Mathieu. He cornered me upstairs a couple of days ago and started trying to tell me about the *sons of Bast*, whoever the hell they are. But as soon as Madame arrived, he was off."

Maggie supped coffee. "I think you're letting your imagination run away with you."

"You don't live there."

"Oh, come on, Gene, the whole thing with Lorie is *genetic*. It's nothing to do with monsters or beast-people or reptiles from twenty thousand fathoms. It's just some genetic accident that a little bit of common sense can easily overcome You've tried psychiatry, and you're about to try surgery. What more can you possibly do?"

Gene looked thoughtful. "I don't know. There's a tension around the place, like something's going to happen, and I can't work out what it is."

"Gene, of *course* there's tension. There's bound to be. But don't you see that once your problems with Lorie are all worked out, all that tension is going to fade away? You can't expect to get over this thing in five minutes."

"Well, no," said Gene. "I guess not."

He sat down again and frowned at his smoldering

cigarette as if the ribboning smoke could give him a clue to his future happiness.

"Look," said Maggie, "if it makes you feel any better, why don't you award me a couple hours off, and I'll go down to the specialist anthropological library and see what I can find you?"

"You don't have to."

"I know I don't have to. But I'd *like* to. Anything to make you realize that Lorie is a beautiful girl with a slight genetic problem, that the Semple family are not the Munsters, and that it's time you stopped worrying. Henry Ness has noticed you're worried, you know. He keeps wondering if you've done something awful you don't want to tell him, like sell the Panama Canal to Fidel Castro."

Gene checked his watch. "Okay, Maggie. Two, maybe three hours. See if you can get back here by three."

"Fine," said Maggie, finishing her coffee. "And Gene?"

"Yes?"

"Remember I loved you once, and I probably still do, and the thing I want for you more than anything else is happiness."

Gene gave her a reassuring grin. "Thanks, Maggie. You're the next best thing to a guardian angel."

At five that evening, Maggie still hadn't returned from the library, and Henry Ness was calling an urgent policy meeting on the twelfth floor. Gene left a note on Maggie's typewriter to phone him at home, and then collected his files and papers together and went upstairs. Walter Farlowe was outside the conference room, sucking on a dead pipe and looking irritated.

"What's up?" asked Gene.

Farlowe sniffed. "A real dilly. The press hasn't got to it yet, but some maniac's kidnapped the son of the French Ambassador."

"You're kidding! You mean today?"

"Last night I guess. The cops are keeping the whole thing shut down tight. It looks like they're expecting some kind of political ransom note or something. Henry's going out of his mind."

"Jesus, I'm not surprised. Do they know who did it yet?"

"Not as far as I know. It seems like they haven't heard anything yet. But Henry thinks it's got something to do with his Middle East initiative. He thinks they're going to put the squeeze on him to lay off the Arabs, on pain of the kid's death."

At that moment, the doors of the conference room were opened, and they were invited in. Henry Ness was already there, along with a dark-suited FBI man, and representatives from the French Embassy and the CIA.

"Now, gentlemen," said Henry Ness, "let's consider what this kidnap's going to mean."

They talked for three hours, going around and around Henry's defensive neuroses about his Middle East discussions, but as the room grew bluer and smokier, and the State Department executives grew wearier and less inspirational, and as the police reported that there was still no news from the kidnappers, the discussions gradually ground to a halt. As Henry was expounding his personal theories about the crime for the fifteenth time, the telephone by Gene's elbow began to ring. "Excuse me sir," he said, and picked it up.

"Keiller."

"Darling, this is Lorie."

"Oh, hi. Listen, honey, I'm right in the middle of it.

We have the Secretary here and we're struck for a couple of hours at least."

"Well, that's okay. The circus doesn't start until nine-thirty."

"Circus? What do you mean?"

"It's a surprise. I managed to book us two tickets for tonight's performance."

He reached for his cigarettes across the table. "Lorie, I hate to tell you this, but I don't think I really want to go."

"But this one sounds so good, darling. Everybody says they have wonderful trapeze artists."

Gene lit his cigarette and rubbed the back of his neck in suppressed exasperation. "Lorie, after spending five hours in conference, I must tell you that the last thing I want to do is go to a circus. Now, will you do me a favor and take the tickets back?"

"Oh, Gene."

"I'm sorry, honey, but I'm too bushed."

"Oh, Gene, I was so looking forward to it."

"Well, maybe some other night."

"All the other nights are booked. Anyway, tonight's special."

"What's special about it?"

"It just is."

Gene could see Henry Ness glaring at him in very thinly disguised disapproval. This was supposed to be the new get-up-and-go administration, and calls from home in the middle of crisis policy meetings were not exactly encouraged. In Henry's view, an executive was married to his desk, and any man who went home to his wife more than a couple of times a week was almost a bigamist, or at the very least an adulterer.

"I have to go," said Gene, "I'm in the middle of a meeting."

"Oh, please say yes."

"Listen, I'll catch you later. We can discuss it then."

"I love you, Gene. Please say yes."

Henry Ness let out a rumbling cough. Gene smirked in embarrassment. "All right, Lorie," he said. "Okay. We'll go. Come around to the office at nine. Now listen, I have to hang up."

"Oh, Gene, you're beautiful. I adore you so much."

"Yes, well, me too. Goodbye now."

Gene laid the receiver down, and turned back to the meeting with an earnest face, as if he'd just taken a call from Castro's foreign minister, or the British Prime Minister.

"Not domestic trouble, I hope, Gene?" Henry Ness asked.

"Oh no, sir. Far from it."

"Good. You people make enough of a mess of things abroad, without doing the same at home."

Everybody laughed loud hyena laughs, and then they got back to the kidnapping.

The circus didn't finish until nearly a quarter of midnight, and Gene was tired and irritable as they walked across the field to the parking lot, through discarded popcorn boxes and half-chewed pizzas. The lights in the tents and sideshows were going out, and the clowns and bareback riders were going back to their trailers to shower, drink a bottle of beer, and watch late-night television.

Gene's raincoat collar was turned up against the chill of the November evening, but his tiredness made him feel cold and shivery. They had been late for the circus because of a snarl-up on the freeway, and then they had found that their reserved seats had been commandeered by an immovable redneck in a plaid lumber jacket and his five, fat children. In the end, they had spent two uncomfortable hours on a wooden form, way back among the coughing and sneezing kids and the senile senior citizens, and everything that had happened in the ring had been invariably inaudible and usually invisible.

Lorie, though, in her long fur coat, seemed particularly glowing and happy; he supposed that if going to the circus did this much to please her, it was a small price to pay. He reached in his pocket and discovered he was out of cigarettes.

"Gene," said Lorie, "I'm so excited."

"Excited? What's to be excited about?"

"Oh, everything. Everything's just so exciting."

"You could have fooled me. All I saw was some fat ladies on horses and a guy getting himself shot a couple of feet in the air out of a cannon.

Lorie tugged his arm so that he stopped walking, and she looked up at him with sparkling eyes.

"Gene, let's go look at the lions."

"The lions? Is that a very good idea?"

"Gene, they were beautiful. Did you see how beautiful they were?"

"Well, sure. They were okay."

"*Okay*? They were *beautiful.* That big male with that fantastic mane. Did you see his face? He's so virile, and wise-looking, but he looks strong and fierce too."

"Lorie, I'm sorry, but I'm just not a connoisseur of lions."

"You married me."

"Sure, but, look, I don't think this is a very good idea, that's all. I think the best thing we can do is get back to the car and go home."

Lorie leaned forward and kissed him. Her lips felt

warm in the chill breeze, and he could smell that distinctive aroma that always clung around her.

"Please, Gene. They're just around the corner."

He looked at her, and she was so lovely that all he could do was smile and say, "All right. A quick couple of minutes. And maybe you can point out some of their finer features to an amateur lion-lover who doesn't know a mane from a floormop."

She kissed him again. "You're perfect," she whispered. "You just don't know how perfect you are."

They walked around the clowns' trailers, past the elephant enclosure until they reached the row of cages where the lions and tigers were kept. It was dark here now, because the generators had been switched off for the night, and the grass rustled in the wind. From the gloom of the cages, Gene heard the scratch of claws of wooden floors, and the deep growling purr of great carnivorous beasts as they slept.

Lorie was pulling him by the hand, and as they came nearer to the cage at the end of the line where the huge male lion was kept, she seemed to tug him along faster and faster, as if she could hardly wait to get there.

Finally, they stood in front of the lion's cage. Lying in the center of the boarded floor, his shaggy head lifted, the lion watched them approach. His slanted eyes closed then widened again, then watched them steadily and with total cruel confidence as they admired him from beyond his bars.

"There," breathed Lorie. "Isn't he beautiful? Isn't he just magnificent?"

Gene squinted into the cage. "He looks fine to me. Yes, he's pretty good-looking."

"Oh, he's more than good-looking," said Lorie, in a hushed, enthralled voice that he had never heard her use before. "He's like a king. He's like a god. Look at those muscles. Look at that gorgeous fur. Look at those claws."

Gene coughed. "I don't know. He seems pretty mangy round the edges. Do you know what I mean?"

Lorie hardly seemed to listen. "He's been caged up, haven't you, my fine brutal darling? He's been locked up for so long. Do you know how much a beautiful lion like that weighs?"

"Two hundred pounds? Come on, Lorie. It's cold. We ought to be going."

The lion growled, and shook its head. Lorie embraced herself in her arms, and closed her eyes.

"Lorie," said Gene, irritably. "It's time we left. I haven't eaten anything all day, except for that lousy hotdog, and I'm about as cold as a polar bear's pickax."

Lorie's eyes stayed closed, and she smoothed the fur on her sleeves as if she was caressing herself. The lion growled again, and lowered its massive head on to its paws.

"Lorie," said Gene. "Will you please say goodbye to your friend and come home?"

Lorie gradually opened her eyes and turned around. "You can't mock him, you know," she whispered. "He may be locked up in a cage, but you can't mock him. He is too magnificent for that."

"Look, I'm not mocking him. What should I want to mock him for? I'm just asking you to come along home."

"Wait. Just one moment."

She stepped right up to the bars of the cage. The lion watched her closely, squeezing its eyes open and shut in narrow slits. Gene was about to warn her about standing so close to the bars, but something inside him said no, she knows what she's doing. She knows exactly what she's doing.

The lion lifted its head again, and then stood up. It was a powerful and fully grown male, dull and out of condition because of its life in a cage but still coursing with muscles and rippling with strength. It had a deep, musky smell about it.

Slowly, its tail swinging, the lion paced up to the bars where Lorie stood. It pulled back its lips in a slight snarl, and growled again, but Lorie stayed where she was. Finally, the beast came right up to her, and sniffed at her tentatively, clawing the floor with its pads. Lorie stood there for a moment, tense and upright, and then she took one step back and bowed. A deep, sweeping bow, almost to the ground.

"Lorie," Gene said, sharply.

She finished her bow and stood straight again. "He's wonderful," she said. "I have to show him that I consider him superb. I have to make my obeisance."

"Obeisance? To a goddamn lion? Lorie, for Christ's sake."

Lorie stiffened. "You're forgetting something, Gene."

"I'm not forgetting anything. I just don't want you making curtseys to any mangy animals, that's all."

Lorie was about to say something, but she contained herself. "All right, Gene," she said quietly, "I'm sorry. But don't forget that I'm half lion myself. This beast is my kin, as well as a beautiful beast."

"Lorie, I know that. Don't you think I've had my nose rubbed in that for a month? But you promised me that you'd try and forget about the lion part of your personality, and relate yourself to human things, to human ideals. This . . . king of the jungle . . . well, he may be terrific as far as lions go, but I don't want you making bows in front of him. Do you get that? He's an animal, and we're humans, and that makes us superior to him. It's nothing to do with kinship. It's a fact of natural history."

Lorie turned back and looked at the lion. She shook her head slowly and the lion growled and settled itself down again.

"Do you understand what I'm saying?" asked Gene.

"Yes," said Lorie, "I understand."

"But you don't agree with me?"

"Do you want me to?"

"I can't force you. But I'd rather you did."

Lorie took his arm, and they walked away from the rows of lion cages and back over the rough grass toward the parking lot. On the cloverleaf, the ceaseless traffic rumbled and roared, and brake lights blinked red through the frosty night.

"Gene," said Lorie, "you won't ever think that I don't love you, will you? You won't ever think that what I feel for you is false?"

"Why should I think that?"

She stopped, and suddenly held him close. "You shouldn't ever think it, because it will never be true. I love you more than you'll ever understand."

He gently kissed her soft hair, and nuzzled against her. He wished he didn't feel so tired.

"As long as you love me more than you love lions," he said quietly.

She raised her head, and looked at him. "There is an expression in the old Ubasti language," she said. "It is *hakhim-al farikka*, and it means 'the two loves in the one love.' One day you will understand what that means, and how strong a love it is."

He kissed her again. "You learn something every day," he said gently. "Come on, let's get home."

At one in the morning, just before he was ready to switch off his bedroom lamp and go to sleep, he remembered Maggie. He picked up the phone by his bed and dialed her number. It rang fifteen or sixteen times before she answered, and she sounded sleepy.

"Hallo," she mumbled.

"I'm sorry," Gene said. "I woke you again."

"Is that you, Gene?"

"Listen, I can call back in the morning."

"No, no," she said quickly. "Don't do that. Just give me a second to wake up."

He picked at his teeth with a match. After they'd come home from the circus, he had made himself a cold beef sandwich, with pickles, and there were shreds stuck in his gums. "Are you all right? You sound kind of strange."

"I'm fine," she said, "but I went down to that library today and I found all kinds of weird stuff."

"Can't it wait until the morning?"

"Well, it could. But there's some things here I think you ought to know. Hold on a moment. Here they are. I found them in a really crusty old book called *Forbidden Religions of the Nile*. There's a whole chapter on the Ubasti, although someone's torn the illustrations out. The librarian reckons they were saucy or something."

Gene coughed. "Does it say anything new? Anything we don't know already?"

"Well, there's a bit here that really worried me," said Maggie. "It goes on about Tell Besta, and the worship of the lion-god Bast, and some of the rituals, which were positively sickening, but there's this bit that says something about their marriages."

"Can you read it?"

"Sure. It says: 'According to the strict command of

the Lion-God Bast, the women of the cult were charged with protecting the species of Ubasti for ever and ever. They were to do this by mating alternately by generations with lions and with humans. In other words, if a Ubasti woman mated with a lion, her daughter would be obliged to mate with a man, and so forth, alternately, thus keeping the strength of this curious mixed race strong, both lion and human."

Gene listened. "That doesn't make sense," he said.

"Why not?"

"Well, Lorie's mother married Jean Semple, who was a human being, and Lorie's married me, and I'm a human being, too."

"You haven't slept with her yet, though, have you? She's not your mate."

"Well, no, but as soon as she's recovered from the plastic surgery——"

"Wait, Gene. Just listen to what it says here. After all this business about carrying on the line by alternately mating with lions and humans, it says this: 'The Ubasti ritual of mating is complex and always carried out strictly according to the divine instructions laid down by the Great Lion-God Bast. If a woman is to mate with a man, then she must offer the man money and jewels, and sacrifice a lion in his name. But if a woman is to mate with a lion, then she must offer to the lion, as his sacrifice, a man."

"Maggie——" interrupted Gene.

"Wait, there's more. Listen to this. 'After a woman has mated with a man, she must preserve the secrecy of her descent and of what has happened by silencing him forever. This is usually done by the lion-woman biting off his tongue.' "

Gene was silent. He could hear Maggie breathing on the other end of the phone. He scratched his forehead carefully; but inside his mind his thoughts were plummeting down a thousand miles of empty uncertainty.

"Are you sure about this?" he asked hoarsely.

"It's in the book. And the book is cross-quoted in several other books that are very respectable and distinguished."

He let out a long breath. "Do you think it's true?" he asked her. "Or do you think that it's just a legend?"

"I don't know, Gene. I'm sorry. I wish I did. I simply thought you ought to know."

"Maggie," he said quietly, "we went to the circus today."

"I thought you hated circuses."

"I do, but Lorie insisted. After it was all over, she took me around to see the lions."

"And?"

He couldn't say it. He couldn't tell even Maggie what was on his mind. But if, as the legend said, it was Lorie's turn to mate with a lion, then the lion was there, waiting for her. And if the words of the book were really true, then she hadn't married Gene for love, or for anything to do with affection or trust or respect. She had deliberately enticed him, wooed him, and married him, so that she could offer him as bait to her real intended mate. Perhaps that was what Mathieu had really meant by "Smith's gazelle." Gene Keiller was Lorie Semple's wedding gift to the beast that was going to father her children.

He laid the phone down numbly in his lap. So much of it fitted together, so logically, that he felt as if the world had been kicked away from under his feet. Maybe Lorie had genuinely loved him at the beginning, and that was why she had tried to discourage him so much. She had known what would happen if they fell in love and married. She had known, even more surely then she knew that she loved him, that she would have to surrender him up as a sacrifice.

In his own blind persistence, he had actually fought his way *into* the trap. As soon as Mrs. Semple had seen him, neither he nor Lorie had stood a chance of *not* getting married. She had cajoled and encouraged Gene to go out with Lorie, and as Lorie's mother and elder in the religion of the Lion-God Bast, she had presumably found it easy to command Lorie to go along with the inevitable ritual.

Between them, Lorie and her mother had done everything they could to keep him at the Semple mansion, and to prepare him for the role he was finally going to have to play. Maybe Lorie's hunt for blood on the night after their wedding had been a mistake, but he could see now how smoothly Mrs. Semple had lulled him into believing that it was all an unfortunate lapse, and that Lorie would soon "get better."

She would never "get better." She was a daughter of the Ubasti, and like all the daughters of the Ubasti, she was committed to the sacred and ancient mission of preserving the race of the Lion-God Bast. It would be easier to try to "rehabilitate" a dedicated Moslem, or a devout Catholic.

"Gene?" said Maggie. "Gene, are you there?"

"Yes, Maggie. I'm here."

"Gene, are you thinking what I've been thinking? I mean, I didn't like to say it, but——"

He coughed. "I don't know, Maggie. It just seems to fit, that's all. It just seems to answer all the questions."

"If it's true, Gene, you ought to get out of there. I mean, quick."

"And what if it isn't?"

"Gene, if they're going to offer you up to some lion, then I don't think you really have the time to quibble."

"But what if it *isn't* true? What if it's some hoary old legend? If I walk out of here now, I'm going to lose Lorie for good. Things are strained enough as it is."

Maggie was silent for a moment. "Why don't you go find Mathieu, and ask him?"

"Mathieu?"

"You remember what he told you about the sons of Bast. Well, doesn't it seem logical that-that's what the sons of Bast are? They're lions, Gene. Actual lions."

"But why should——"

He stopped himself. He frowned. "Maggie," he said, "read that bit again. That bit about preserving the secrecy of the lion-people."

Maggie shuffled papers, and then read: " 'After a woman has mated with a man, she must preserve the secrecy of her descent and of what has happened by silencing him for ever. This is usually done by the lion-woman biting off his tongue.' "

Gene listened, and then nodded. "It makes sense, doesn't it?" he said quietly.

"What did you say?"

"It all fits. Mathieu isn't Mathieu at all. He's Lorie's father. Can you get me a photograph of Jean Semple from the newspaper morgue first thing tomorrow? If it isn't Mathieu, then I don't know who the hell it is."

"But if he knows about the lion-people, if they actually bit off his tongue, surely he would have tried to escape?"

"Maybe he would," said Gene. "But on the other hand, maybe he wouldn't. What's a mute diplomat going to do to keep himself in business? Maybe it was easier to stay at the house and have Lorie's mother look after him. Maybe he still loves her. I think the best thing I can do is go find him and ask him for myself."

"Gene," said Maggie worriedly, "do you have a gun there?"

"Sure. I have a 30–30 big-game rifle."

"Well, please take care. I mean it. Call me if you need help, and I'll get round there right away."

"I think I can manage. Can you try to stay by the phone?"

"Surely. Let me know when you've talked to Mathieu."

"I will. And, well, thanks, Maggie. That's all I can say."

"Don't say anything, Gene. Just stay alive."

He lifted the rifle out from under the bed and made sure it was loaded. It was a quarter after one now, and the house was very quiet and dark. Yesterday's wind had blown itself out, and the night seemed suspended in stillness and silence. Only the haunted cry of owls in the woods disturbed the sleep of the Semple estate and its shadowy house; and only Gene's tautened breathing disturbed the absolute tension of his bedroom.

He dressed in a roll-neck sweater and dark gray slacks. Then he took the rifle in his right hand and went softly to the door. He opened it, and it creaked. The landing outside was deserted and dark.

He knew that Mathieu slept downstairs someplace, but he didn't know exactly where. Treading as lightly as he could, he tiptoed along the landing until he reached the head of the stairs. Behind him, the stained glass window washed pale colored light into the gloom of the house. He waited, and listened, but there was no sound at all.

Keeping his hand on the banister rail, he stepped slowly downstairs. The hallway was so dark that he had to wait at the foot of the stairs so that his eyes could gradually grow accustomed to the shadows. When he was ready, he walked across to the kitchen door and pushed it open. He was pretty sure that Mathieu had a room that came off the scullery someplace.

The kitchen door squeaked, and he held his breath for thirty seconds waiting to hear if he had awakened anyone. Lorie he didn't mind about. He knew she was asleep and locked in. But it was Mrs. Semple who was the unknown factor. If the legends that Maggie had read to him were grounded anywhere in fact, Mrs. Semple was a powerful and dominent figure in this household, and she was dedicated to the preservation of her species. That didn't make for a friendly opponent, or any tolerance about snooping around the house in the dark.

The house was still quiet, so he walked softly across the kitchen to the scullery door. It was a few inches ajar, and he pushed it a little further open with the muzzle of his rifle. Beyond the door, it was totally dark, and he would have to make his way by feel.

With one hand raised to protect himself from colliding with unseen furniture, and the rifle held upright in the other hand, Gene shuffled gently toward the left side of the scullery, where he guessed that Mathieu's room was. He paused every now and then to listen, but it seemed that everything was still quiet.

He was just about to put his hand on the doorknob of Mathieu's room when he thought he heard a slight scuffling noise. He froze, and tensed. Silence. He reached out again for the doorknob, and then something hit him a bruising blow across the neck, something as hard and violent as a bar of iron. He fell against the wall, lost his balance, and crashed to the floor. His rifle was twisted out of his hand and skated across the scullery.

A heavy body dropped on top of him, and a callused hand was clamped over his mouth. He twisted around and tried to get away, but his assailant was far too powerful for him.

"Don't move," croaked a deep, aspirate voice. "Don't move once, I break your neck."

Gene lay still. The back of his head had hit the tiled floor of the scullery, and it was almost blinding him with pain.

He mumbled, "Monsieur Semple?"

There was a long silence. Then the heavy body was eased off him, and the hand taken away from his face.

"You know me?" said the wheezing, hollow voice. "You know me?"

Gene lifted himself up on one elbow and gently touched the bruise at the back of his head.

"I guessed," he said quietly. "Based on anthropological evidence."

"You know about Ubasti?"

"Not until tonight. My secretary's been doing some research for me in the specialist anthropological library. She dug up all the stuff about breeding by alternate generations."

"Smith's gazelle," croaked M. Semple.

"That's right," said Gene. "Smith's gazelle. Tonight I worked out who the gazelle was and what I was here for."

M. Semple reached out a hand and helped Gene to his feet. "You must come into my room," he said hoarsely. "We must not wake the ladies."

He pushed open the door next to the scullery, and ushered Gene into a small bed-sitting room. There was a single, untidy bed with a red bedspread, a long, makeshift shelf of books, and two threadbare armchairs. The room was heated by a tiny electric fire with a tarnished reflector, and the only other comfort was a hotplate where M. Semple could apparently brew coffee and tea. The walls were hung with dozens of framed photographs of French officers in Tunis and Algeria, photographs of Mrs. Semple, and pictures of Lorie when she was a baby.

"Sit down," invited M. Semple. "I am sorry I hit you. I have to protect myself."

Gene sat down. "Do you have any cigarettes?"

"If you don't mind Gauloises. I'm allowed one hundred a week."

Gene took a French cigarette out of the blue pack that M. Semple offered him, and soon the room was clouded with the pungent smell of *tabac*. M. Semple sat down opposite and crossed his legs. He was still as impassive and hard-faced as usual, but for the first time Gene noticed that his impassiveness seemed to reflect his internal thoughtfulness and self-secrecy, rather than an aggressive attitude toward the world around him.

"You speak well," said Gene. "Did you teach yourself?"

M. Semple nodded. "After the she-lion bit out my tongue, I could not speak at all for months. But I read in *Time* magazine about men who had their larynx removed, and how they learned to speak again, and I taught myself. It is hard effort, of course, and I do not let those she-lions know that I can do it very much. One day, I will need to speak by surprise."

"You surprised me."

"The feeling is mutual, Mr. Keiller. I thought you were going to go to your fate like an obedient gazelle."

"You knew what they had in mind?"

"Of course."

"Then why didn't you tell me before?"

"I tried to give you clues. But they are always watching, those she-lions. If they knew that we have spoken, they will tear me to pieces."

"What about the police?"

"Mr. Keiller, I wish to survive. I am afraid that my feelings about you were that if you were foolish enough to walk into this lair with your eyes open, and wait for your sacrificial death without a murmur, then that was your own affair."

It took M. Semple a long time to say this, and he had to pause for rest in between sentences, but Gene was amazed at the clarity of his curious organ-pipe voice. He must have spent hours and hours every night, training his voice by do-it-yourself speech therapy. There were several books on diction and voice training on his shelf.

"M. Semple," he said, "can you try and tell me what's going on here? Can you try and tell me what Lorie and Mrs. Semple are actually doing?"

M. Semple lit a cigarette for himself. "They are not doing anything they consider out of the ordinary. They are simply carrying on the line of the Lion-God Bast."

"But how can they persuade a lion to . . . how can they get it to mate?"

M. Semple's face remained expressionless. "There is a ritual, which is always observed. It dates back to the days of Tell Besta, which I presume you know about. When Rameses cast out the worshippers of the Lion-God Bast from the Upper Nile, and cursed them forever in the name of Horus, the worshippers swore that they would continue the line of lion-people for ever more. The name of Bast would never die. And, sure enough, after all these centuries, it has not."

The Frenchman paused for breath, and to puff at his

cigarette. "When it is the generation of the lion-mating, when it is time for a girl to have intercourse with a lion, they go through the same procedure. The girl herself goes out and selects a choice human tidbit for the lion's sacrificial gift. It is important that this gift is a virile and intelligent male, and that is why Lorie went to the party—to choose someone. You, regrettably, chose yourself; and it was a pity because Lorie actually liked you, and in a very short time, grew to love you. She did not want the sacrifice to be you. But you, very stubbornly, seemed determined to offer yourself up to Bast. Once my wife had seen you, she considered you perfect, and that is why they have done so much to keep you here."

"What about the night that Lorie went out and killed that sheep? Surely that was a risk. That almost put me off her once and for all."

"It is something that happens," wheezed M. Semple. "They cannot help it. As the lion-mating draws closer, the lioness within them grows irresistibly stronger, and they prowl around at night like real lions. They cannot prowl by day because they are cursed by the sun-god Horus, and if they did so they would die. A few weeks before the lion-mating, the Ubasti girl goes out and anoints herself, in preparation, with the blood of a first-born child. That is done to prove to herself that she is enough of a lioness at heart, and that the strain of the lion-people flows strongly enough in her veins."

"You mean . . ."

"There was no sheep. Your suspicions were quite right. She went out that night, mauled a young boy to death, and devoured him."

Gene dropped his eyes. "Oh, Christ," he said quietly. "And to think I believed her."

M. Semple shrugged. "It was not your fault. You

had good faith and trust in your wife. I am her father, remember, Mr. Keiller, and I knew that if only she were normal, she would have an exemplary husband in you."

Gene drew deep at his cigarette. "Thank you, M. Semple. I only wish I could say that was a consolation."

M. Semple stood up, and walked across to the photographs on the wall. "This is my wife on the day we were married. Isn't she beautiful? If only I had known what was to come."

"M. Semple, the other night, I thought I saw a kind of . . . I don't know, *shape* . . . leaving the house in the dark. I couldn't be sure. I checked up on Lorie, and she was still in her room."

M. Semple nodded. "That was my wife. As a lion-priestess, she is duty-bound to tempt the lion to mate with her daughter. One temptation is you, of course, the main sacrifice. You will be offered to the lion after mating, and the lion will devour you. You and the lion will then be in what they call a state of *hakhim-al farikka,* 'two loves in one.' But of course the lion has to be tempted to the mating place, too, and this is done by finding a boy-child and ripping him open alive, so that his blood and entrails can be dragged as a trail along the ground to the mating-place."

Gene frowned. "You mean, *another* boy has been killed?"

M. Semple nodded. "Last night. He was the son of the French Ambassador. My wife, of course, knows the French Embassy well, and all who live and work there. It was a simple matter for her to steal the boy at night."

"I can't believe it. I simply can't believe it. Are you

telling me that the boy was dragged out of his bed by Mrs. Semple and *killed*. Just to make a *trail*?"

"You don't have to believe it," said M. Semple. "But I thought you would have seen enough by now to convince you that it is true. These are the she-lions of Ubasti, Mr. Keiller. They are the most terrible creatures on this earth, and always have been, since the days of Rameses and all the pharaohs."

Gene crushed out his Gauloise. "But if you knew this, why didn't you try to do something? Anything?"

M. Semple sat down on the end of his bed. He pulled at the fraying tassels of his bed-cover. "Perhaps you will think I am a coward. Yes, I am. I have learned to keep myself quiet and do what I am told. It is the only way in which I can survive. I cannot escape this place. If I tried to get away even once, the she-lions would find me, and they would tear me to shreds."

"You'd rather let two young kids die than——"

M. Semple raised his head. "You don't have to remind me of how ashamed I feel, Mr. Keiller. There are times when I could cut my throat for shame. But the Ubasti bring nothing but death wherever they go. It was like in Canada, when another man died because of me. A vagrant from Vancouver. My wife dressed him in my clothes, and then ripped him apart so that he was unrecognizable. She later said the body was mine, and that was how I 'died.' The Ubasti are cold-blooded, Mr. Keiller, and your choice is either to die like a sheep or survive like a rat."

"You've got guns, for Christ's sake. Why the hell don't you pick up that big-game rifle and blow their heads off?"

M. Semple grunted in amusement. "Guns, Mr. Keiller, but no live ammunition. They gave you that 30–30 to make you feel secure. That's all. The rounds are blank."

Gene stood up, and brushed ash from his clothes. "M. Semple," he said, "I'm getting out of here right now. I'm leaving. And the first thing I'm going to do when I get out is call the police."

"I cannot let you," said M. Semple, with no expression.

"You'll have to try and stop me."

"I can stop you. I am an expert in kravmaga. I was trained by the Israelis in the Middle East."

"M. Semple, you don't understand. If I call the cops, we can get you out of here, and have Lorie and your wife put away."

M. Semple shook his head. "You Americans are all the same. Cops and robbers! You don't understand the carnage that would happen. And what about me, anyway? I am as much to blame for those boys' death as they are. What do they call it? Accessory to murder. I am an accessory."

"M. Semple, I'm going."

"Don't try, Mr. Keiller. You will only die a worse death. Better to let it happen easily and quickly. They will catch you long before you reach the gates. And anyway, the lion will be on his way, too, from the circus."

Gene paused. "Lion?" he said, uneasily.

"That is correct. Last night, my wife dragged the trail from the circus to the house. Tonight is the chosen night for the lion-mating. It has to be early, you see, because the circus changed its plans."

Gene suddenly remembered Mrs. Semple at dinner. "Stay for one more week," she had said. "Give Lorie seven more days. Then you'll discover just how much things have changed."

"In that case, the sooner I get out of this place, the better."

He opened the door. For a moment, M. Semple sat on the end of his bed motionless, but as Gene tried to step through the door, he lashed out with astonishing swiftness with his right leg and slammed the door shut.

Gene backed off. He clenched his fists and assumed the boxing pose they had taught him at school. M. Semple moved cautiously around him, watching him with eyes that didn't even give away the fact that he was alive.

"Come on, M. Semple," said Gene. "You and me together, we can beat them. Why fight between ourselves?"

M. Semple shook his head. "Because you are no match for a lion, that is why. I know where the odds are stacked. I am sorry, Mr. Keiller, but you cannot go."

Gene ducked forward but M. Semple hit him a flat-handed chop on the side of the head that made his ears ring. He staggered, but managed to stay on his feet, and dodged behind one of the armchairs. They were both panting now, and they feinted and weaved, their eyes fixed on each other, their muscles tense.

With a fast-moving heave, Gene pushed the armchair forward into M. Semple's shins, and then threw himself against the back of it with all his weight. M. Semple was forced back for a moment, and that moment was enough for Gene to whip open the door and dive into the darkness of the scullery.

M. Semple tossed the armchair aside as if it weighed as little as a pillow, and he came hurtling after Gene so fast that Gene hardly had time to turn around and face him in the confines of the tiny room.

"You make a mistake," panted M. Semple. "You cannot escape. I am sorry, but no way."

He lashed out a kick that hit Gene right in the stomach. Gene folded up, winded and hurt, and pitched on his shoulder to the floor. He landed almost on top of the rifle.

"Now, then, Mr. Keiller, please get up," said M. Semple. "Please make it easy. Any more noise will waken the she-lions."

Gene knelt there, gasping to get some air back in his lungs. Then his hand touched the rifle in the darkness. He reached for the trigger, and then paused for a few seconds, still fighting for breath, until he could sense that M. Semple had relaxed.

He was going to have to be quick. Incredibly quick. He was going to have to do this so fast and accurate that M. Semple wouldn't even realize what was happening.

He counted—five, four, three, two, one—and then he bunched his muscles and swung the rifle up to M. Semple's face, so that the muzzle was only an inch away from his eyes. He pulled the trigger.

It was only a blank, but there was a blast of powder and cardboard packing that blinded M. Semple in a deafening report. The Frenchman fell backwards with a hoarse scream, and lay twitching on the floor with his hands over his eyes.

"Aaaahhhhhh, *mes yeux, mes yeux . . . au secours, mes yeux . . .*"

Gene dropped the rifle with a noisy clatter and pushed his way out of the scullery. He knew it was wrong to leave M. Semple like that, but his she-lions would find him soon enough. Right now, the most urgent priority was to get out of the Semple estate as fast as possible.

He ran through the kitchen, and banged open the door into the hallway with both hands. The front door was only three steps away on his right. Three bolts, one heavy lock, and then he would be free. He slammed the kitchen door behind him and hurried across the tiled floor.

The first bolt shot back easily. The second was a little more stiff. But it was while he was wrestling to free it that he thought he heard something behind him. A rumbling noise, low and menacing. A scratching of long nails on bare wood.

He turned around. A few yards away, the stairs rose upwards towards the stained-glass window. Halfway down the stairs, lithe, terrifying and pale in the gloom, and naked and pale and, poised on all fours like the lion-people they were, he saw Lorie and Mrs. Semple. Their tawny hair was wild, and their eyes were as glinting and cold as the lion he had seen at the circus. Their lips were pulled back in a snarl of surprise and vicious anger.

Step by step, they loped head-first down the stairs, and padded across the hallway toward him, growling and tossing their heads. Their teeth were yellow and curved and sharp, and he knew then that there was nothing human or forgiving about them at all.

Eight

He banged back the second and third bolts and turned the key in a split-second surge of fear and adrenalin. The she-lions saw what he was doing. Lorie bounded toward him faster, and then launched herself into a snarling leap.

Gene rolled himself to one side, and Lorie landed heavily on the floor like a cat, her nails scratching and sliding on the tiles. Gene wrenched open the door, and pushed his way out into the night, tearing his sweater on the doorkey. He closed his eyes and ran away from the house, up the gravel drive, faster than he'd ever run before.

He heard the loping sound of the two Ubasti women behind him, as they ran easily and swiftly in pursuit. The gates were still a hundred and fifty yards away, and he knew that he wasn't going to make it. They were too strong and too fast, and they were bred to kill.

His legs pumped up and down, and the breath hit his lungs in scorching gasps. The oak trees along the driveway joggled past his vision like a blur of *cinéma vérité*. Ahead of him, as he rounded the corner in the drive, he could see the tall iron gates, and he hoped and prayed to God that there was some way to get them open.

It wasn't long, though, before he saw a pale shape flickering alongside of him behind the rows of oaks.

One of the she-lions had caught up, and was running level. She would only have to cut across now, and his escape would be diverted, and closed off. Not far behind him, he heard the other one's bare hands and feet beating out a four-legged rhythm on the gravel, and he could hear the beast-woman's breath coming closer and closer.

Desperately, he tried to run through the long grass and through the oaks and make his way toward the place where he had scaled the wall in his first search for Lorie. Perhaps, with a shadow of luck, the rope he had used would still be there. He knew that he couldn't run for very much longer, and if he miscalculated, and reached the wall at the wrong point, he was going to be finished.

He leaped and jumped through tangles of briars and tree-roots, and ran and ran across the open lawns. To his left, the pale shape of the she-lion was still almost level, and now he could see the other one running to his right. They were hunting him down in just the way that lionesses hunt zebra and antelope in the African bush. While he was trying to get away from them by calculating the best place to go, they were tracking him down by instinct.

He knew that he wasn't going to make the wall. He was heaving for breath, and his legs were leaden and stumbling and didn't seem to cooperate at all. The lawn he was running across went upward in a long gentle slope, a very gentle slope, but enough to drag him to a standstill. He was staggering by the time he got anywhere near the trees, and the she-lions were running in faster and faster to catch him.

There was a sound like paws bounding through leaves. He lifted his arm to protect himself. Then Lorie leaped at him from the left, and her weight dropped him straight to the leafy ground, rolling him over and pinning him helplessly against the roots of a tree.

He closed his eyes. He waited for the jaws to bite into him. He could hear Lorie panting and slavering saliva, and he could feel the pressure of her body on top of him, and there was that rank lion-like smell around.

Tentatively, he opened his eyes and looked up. Lorie saw him, and shifted away. She crouched a little way off, watching him with her beautiful and animal face, and purring deeply. Her mother came running through the trees and joined her, and together they sat staring at him, so remote and leonine that it was hard for him to think that they had ever been people. He had danced with this girl, taken her to parties, talked with her, laughed with her, and yet here she was, naked and wild in a November wood, guarding him with a hostile stare and bared teeth.

Guarding him, that's what they were doing. He understood that now. They weren't going to kill him because he was their prize sacrifice, their human offering to the godly son of Bast who was soon going to arrive to mate with Lorie. They would never dare to devour him. He was Lorie's chance to become a proud mother in the tradition of the Ubasti descent.

Gene lifted himself up a little. "Lorie?" he said, in a coaxing voice. "Can you hear me?"

Lorie tossed her head like a lion tossing away irritating flies, and said nothing.

"Listen, Lorie," said Gene, "you have to believe that you can't do this. The cops are on their way. I promise you that. I called the cops just now and they're coming. If they catch you, Lorie, you're going to go to prison for a long, long time. No lion-babies for you, Lorie. If you don't let me free now, they'll lock you up and they'll take your baby away from you, and probably drown it."

Lorie bared her teeth again, but he wasn't at all sure if she'd understood. He sat up a few inches more, and both she-lions snarled together and moved threateningly toward him. He raised his hands to show that he wasn't going to take any more liberties, and they retreated.

Gene tried to make himself as comfortable as he could. The son of Bast, the lion from the circus, must be expected soon, otherwise they wouldn't be waiting here so patiently. He wondered how the lion was going to get out of its cage. Maybe Mrs. Semple had already fixed the lock or maybe the beast was just going to burst its way straight through the wooden walls. He wished he had a cigarette. Even men condemned to hang can have a last cigarette.

It was cold and still out in the grounds of the Semple estate, but neither of the two lion-women seemed to feel chilled. They sat quietly and placidly side by side, their heads lifted to catch any sound of Lorie's approaching mate.

"Lorie," urged Gene, for a second time. "Let me go, Lorie. That's all you have to do. Give me a half-hour start. I won't tell a soul about you and your mother, I promise. You can have your lion without me, can't you? Why involve me?"

Lorie stared at him with her green, intense eyes, but she still didn't answer. Mrs. Semple twitched her head uneasily, as if she was worried that the lion from the circus wouldn't show. It had to be touch and go for a beast like that to break out of its cage and run through the suburbs of Merriam without being spotted by police or circus folk. Gene squinted down at his watch and saw it was almost two.

By two-thirty, he was stiff and cramped. The night sky was clouding over, and a soft breeze was rising. Gene started to cough, and tried to shift himself yet again on the bony tree-roots, but Mrs. Semple turned to him and bared her fangs so threateningly that he froze, and stayed where he was.

Then they heard it. The soft, heavy sound of an animal leaping over the wall. The quick running of paws through leaves. Lorie stiffened, and turned her head, and Mrs. Semple rose up on to her hands and feet, and started pacing in a nervous figure-of-eight.

There was a rumbling roar. Gene twisted his head around, and there it was. The magnificent son of Bast. It looked even bigger than it had in the cage, and it came stalking across toward them with pride and dignity and a rippling movement that spoke of unstoppable muscular strength. Gene had seen plenty of photographs of circus people and unwary safari-park visitors being mauled by lions, and he had always wondered why they never broke free and ran away. When he saw the sheer size of this fully grown male lion, he understood why.

The lion stopped, and looked slowly around the clearing where they were gathered. It roared once, and to Gene's horror, Lorie roared back, in a strained, baying, on-heat kind of bitch-lion's voice. The lion raised its nose, and Gene saw its black nostrils dilate as it sniffed out Lorie's mating-scent.

Lorie clawed and fretted at the ground. She was grinding her teeth, and her whole body was tense with sexual arousal. The lion paced slowly around her, sniffing cautiously at her hair and her body and between her legs. Mrs. Semple stayed away, lying down in the tangled grass with her head lifted, and Gene was pretty sure that if he tried to make a break for it, she'd be straight after him.

The sniffing and prowling continued for almost ten minutes, as Lorie and her lion-mate got to know each other. They rubbed faces together, and Gene couldn't miss the expression of ecstasy that Lorie had when she nuzzled against the tawny fur of her animal lover. She was intensely sexually aroused, far more than he'd ever seen her before, and she could hardly keep herself from tearing at the turf with her nails in the frenzy of her excitement.

"Gene," she had said at the circus. "I'm so excited."

He heard a rustling noise. It was only when Lorie turned around, and he saw her glistening thighs, that he understood what had happened. She had urinated, so that the odor of her urine would arouse her mate. The lion growled, and sniffed at her, and began to lift himself up behind her.

Lorie was tall and strong, but the male lion was enormous. She stood there on all fours, with her back arched, as the huge shaggy beast raised itself up on her, its red lion-penis quivering, and tried to penetrate her half-human body.

He heard her scream. It was a high-pitched, unnatural scream, more like an animal than a girl, but all the same it was the scream of someone badly hurt. The lion had dug its hooked claws into her shoulders, so that the blood ran down her pale arms. Then it forced itself deeper and deeper inside her, and jerked its sinewy body in the frenzied grip of animal coupling.

Gene felt nausea rising in his throat, but he couldn't look away. Thrust after thrust, the lion worked itself in Lorie's body up toward ejaculation; and then, with an uncontrolled shudder, it shot the lion-sperm into her, immediately dropped back, and turned away with a rumbling growl.

Lorie collapsed on the ground, bleeding and shaking. The male lion circled around her, but it was plain that he wasn't interested in her any more. What he wanted now was his promised sacrifice. What he wanted was raw meat and flesh, and that was why Gene was there.

Gene lifted himself up as high as he could without attracting attention. He had his breath back now, and even if he couldn't run as fast as a lion, he could probably make it to the wall if he had a good start.

He was waiting for the prowling lion to circle around the other side of Lorie, and then he was going to make a break for it.

But, just as he was about to pick himself up and run, the lion stopped circling and raised its huge head. Mrs. Semple turned, too, as if she was listening for something.

There *was* something. Someone was stumbling across the lawns crying out as they came. Gene peered through the shadows, and through the oaks, he saw a figure, blindly crashing through the twigs and the branches, and hoarsely shouting out: *"Lorie! Lorie! Ce'st ton père! Lorie, ma chère! Ma petite! C'est ton père!"*

The lion moved off with frightening speed. It ran slowly at first, but as it crossed the lawns it was running quicker and quicker. M. Semple, blinded by the discharge of Gene's rifle, couldn't even see it coming, although he could probably hear it. It was as fast and as heavy as a small car, and it seized his right leg in its jaws in one barreling bound. Even from where he was lying, Gene could hear sinews tearing, and the lion guzzled and snapped and growled as it wrenched the

Frenchman this way and that, tearing at his legs and his belly and biting savagely into his face.

Gene heaved himself up, and ran.

Mrs. Semple, who was alertly watching the lion, didn't notice him for the first few seconds. But then she turned and saw him sprinting as hard as he could toward the wall, brushing the twigs and branches away from his face as he ran. With a snarl, she turned around and began to run swiftly after him, trying to cut him off from the wall by running at an angle.

The wall was further than he'd thought. From where he was lying, it had only looked like thirty or forty yards, but now it seemed to be miles away, through the thickest brambles and weeds. He caught his ankle on a root, and it pulled off his shoe, so that he was running on one bruised, stockinged foot. His second wind was giving out, too, and he was snatching at the air for breath.

He could hear her, the running she-lion. She was very close. This time, she knew that he was trying to make his final break, and she was loping after him at full speed. He could even hear her deep, even panting.

He was going so fast that he collided with the wall when he reached it and banged his head. The rope wasn't there—he must have misjudged by fifty or sixty yards. He turned quickly, and he could see the white, lithe shape of Mrs. Semple running toward him, only twenty yards away. He sucked in a deep breath and began to sprint alongside the wall to the place where he thought he might have left the rope. He trailed his fingers against the wall in case he missed it in the darkness.

Mrs. Semple cut across the corner, through the bushes, and made up ten yards of ground. She was snarling now, and when he glanced over his shoulder he could see her glittering eyes and her drawn-back mouth with its razor-sharp teeth.

Something in his mind said: it's no good. The rope's not there. You're never going to make it. She's only twenty feet behind you now, and you're never going to make it.

He squeezed his eyes tight shut, lowered his head, and surged as much strength into his running legs as he could. He ran so fast that he even gained a couple of feet on Mrs. Semple. But he knew he didn't have the stamina or the training to last out. Any second now his body was going to say no, and that would be the end.

His trailing hand touched the rop. The rope!

He slowed to a stop, and scrabbled at the rope for a grip. Shrieking for breath, exhausted and sweating, he pulled himself upward, kicking against the wall to help him scale the bricks. And at that moment, in a streak of pale viciousness, Mrs. Semple reached him and leaped up at his legs.

He kicked her, very hard, in the face. It was his stockinged foot, and he felt the wool tear on her teeth, and he knew that she'd drawn blood. Swinging around on the rope, frantically trying to keep his grip, he kicked her again, and this time she dropped back for a second to give herself the ground to spring up at him again.

With two or three massive heaves on the rope, Gene reached the top of the wall. He felt Mrs. Semple's claw-like nails ripping at his calf muscle, but he lashed out once more, and she fell back. He carefully stood up on the top of the spiked coping-stones, balancing for a moment, and then jumped into the welcome darkness of the grass environs of the estate.

He rolled over, hitting his knee, but he was able to pull himself up to his feet and run through the verge on to the roadway. Only a quarter mile away he saw lights, and that meant safety. Coughing and spitting phlegm, he started to trot along the road toward them.

Halfway down the road, he could see that the lights were coming from the sitting room window of a large, white colonial house. He could see the cars parked in the driveway outside, and the hedges around the front garden, and he could even make out people moving about the room. His trot slowed to a fast walk. He was almost there.

But had not reckoned with the speed of the lions. As he walked quickly toward the lighted house, he heard a pattering noise behind him on the asphalt surface of the road. He turned his head, and only a hundred yards away in the darkness he saw Lorie and her male lion, running toward him with tireless strides, side by side.

"Oh, God," he whispered, and started to run. But he was so exhausted from climbing the wall that he could hardly make his legs move. The house, which had seemed so near, suddenly seemed a mile away. He couldn't stop himself from coughing, and that slowed him up even more. He regretted every damned cigarette he'd ever smoked right then. His lungs felt as if they'd been washed out with blazing kerosene.

He was fifteen feet from the hedge around the house when they caught him. The lion didn't spring on him right away, but circled around him, growling and snarling, and Lorie circled around him too, spitting viciously, her bare hands and feet padding on the roadway.

Gene shambled to a stop, and froze. He raised his left arm a little way to protect himself, in case the lion leaped at his face, but knew how useless it was.

"Lorie," he said hoarsely. "Lorie, for God's sake."

Lorie just snapped at him, her curved teeth shining

in the light from the house. My God, thought Gene, I'm twenty feet away from safety and civilization. Those people are going to come out here to walk their dog tonight and find me ripped apart and strewn all over like that poor nine-year-old kid. He felt more desperate and panicky than he could ever remember.

"Lorie, please! Lorie, listen will you! I know you're Lorie! I know you're in there someplace! Call it off, Lorie! For Christ's sake Lorie, call it off!"

The huge male lion stepped back, its body tensing ready to spring. Its eyes slitted as it focused on him, and its massive jaws pulled back ready to tear his flesh away from his bones.

"Lorie!" screamed Gene. "Lorie, call this monster off me! Lorie, I love you! Call him off!"

Lorie ran around him, and growled at the male lion. The male lion hesitated for a moment, its muscles relaxing. It lifted its proud, enormous head and looked away, almost as if it was too disdainful to be bothered with Lorie, or even with Gene.

Gene stayed right where he was, trying to keep himself from trembling. "Lorie," he whispered. "Please, Lorie. If you ever felt anything for me. Please."

The lion made a half-hearted jump in Gene's direction, and Gene couldn't help jerking nervously back, but Lorie butted the lion with her head, affectionately and gently, and the beast turned away in mid-jump. Then, without any further hesitation, it turned around and began to run off, at a measured and even pace, along the road.

Gene watched it go. In a few moments, it was out of sight in the darkness. He turned around, and Lorie had gone, too, but he didn't know where. He slowly and painfully walked along the length of the hedge around the house, and pushed open the front gate. He went up the neat path to the bright green front door, and knocked.

He waited two or three minutes before the door was answered. Then it opened up, and a tall gray-haired man in an expensive suit stood there with a martini in his hand.

"Well, hi," he said expansively. "What happened to you?"

"Lions," Gene said, and collapsed.

He went, out of a strange sense of compulsion, to Mathieu's funeral. It was a dry, bitterly cold day, and there weren't many people there. The leaves had curled up under foot, and they crunched as they walked toward the grave like soldiers walking through Post Toasties. The sky was clean and blue, and the few wispy clouds were very high up.

Both Mrs. Semple and Lorie were stànding by the grave. They were tall, and together, and dressed in black, with veils over their beautiful faces. The gravestone was simple, and probably hadn't cost very much. It read: Mathieu Besta, From His Loving Friends.

Gene had come late, parking his white New Yorker by the cemetery gate. Maggie came with him, wearing a smart, new black coat that he had bought her specially. They came up the sloping path toward the funeral party, and nobody looked their way. There was a feeling that, remotely and perhaps unfairly, they were unwelcome guests.

The priest was just finishing the service. Mrs. Semple reached down, took a handful of cold dry mud, and threw it on the lid of the coffin. Lorie stood there, silent and unmoving, with her hands across her stomach as if she was already heavily pregnant.

"She's very beautiful," whispered Maggie. "I don't think I've ever seen her this close."

"Beauty," said Gene, "is very often skin deep, and no further."

Maggie frowned at him. "I can tell you're a politician. You talk in clichés."

He smiled absently. "Someone else said that to me, a long time ago."

Mrs. Semple and Lorie left the graveside without even looking his way. Whatever they had between them was now in the hands of attorneys, and Gene had already been told that Lorie would agree to a painless and inexpensive divorce. All she had asked for was sufficient money to support a child, if, as she suspected, she was pregnant.

Gene and Maggie stood there a little while longer, and then walked back down the path to the car.

"You know something," said Gene, as they drove back into the morning sunlight toward Washington.

"What's that?"

"It's always the people who can't defend themselves who get the blame."

"People? Or animals?"

"In this case, animal. Singular."

"But he did kill M. Semple. Or Mathieu Besta, or whatever they wanted to call him."

"Sure. But who let him out? He was nothing but a dumb beast. He probably would have preferred to stay in his cage for the rest of his life, coming out now and again to get prodded by some ringmaster, and retire with grace and dignity and false teeth."

"I don't know how you can laugh about teeth after what you went through."

Gene shrugged. "To tell you to truth, it doesn't seem too real these days."

"Is that why you came today?"

"Maybe. I felt some kind of responsibility, too. I sometimes think that if it hadn't been for me, that poor guy would still be alive."

Maggie took off her black straw hat. "Sure. And you'd be dead."

Gene slowed the New Yorker up for a red light. The morning sun cut across the car, and lit up Maggie's hair. Across the street, tattered and faded, was a poster for Romero's Traveling Circus, with a vivid picture of a lion leaping through a hoop. In the next car, a pale-green Buick, a man with a snap-brim hat was arguing with his wife, his cigarette waggling between his lips.

"Maggie?" Gene said.

"Yes?"

"Would you think I was out of line if I asked you to stay around?"

Maggie turned to him and smiled. "As long as you're not on the rebound," she laughed.

KEILLER, Lorie Semple. To Mrs. Lorie Semple Keiller, former wife of Gene Keiller, of Merriam, Maryland, a girl, Sabina, at Sisters of Mercy Hospital, Merriam. *Hakhim-al Jarikka.*

STAR BOOKS BESTSELLERS

FICTION

SHATTER	John Farris	£1.50*
REVENGE OF MORIARTY	John Gardner	£2.25
GOLGOTHA	John Gardner	£1.95
BACK OF THE TIGER	Jack Gerson	£1.95
SPECTRE OF MARALINGA	Michael Hughes	£1.95
DEBT OF HONOUR	Adam Kennedy	£1.95
DEATH MAIL	Peter Leslie	£1.95
CONDOR	Thomas Luke	£2.50*
AIRSHIP	Peter MaCalan	£2.50
IKON	Graham Masterton	£2.50*
HAWL	James Peacock	£1.95
DOG SOLDIERS	Robert Stone	£1.95

STAR Books are obtainable from many booksellers and newsagents. If you have any difficulty tick the titles you want and fill in the form below.

Name ______________________________

Address ______________________________

____

Send to: Star Books Cash Sales, P.O. Box 11, Falmouth, Cornwall, TR10 9EN.

Please send a cheque or postal order to the value of the cover price plus: UK: 55p for the first book, 22p for the second book and 14p for each additional book ordered to the maximum charge of £1.75.

BFPO and EIRE: 55p for the first book, 22p for the second book, 14p per copy for the next 7 books, thereafter 8p per book.

OVERSEAS: £1.00 for the first book and 25p per copy for each additional book.

While every effort is made to keep prices low, it is sometimes necessary to increase prices at short notice. Star Books reserve the right to show new retail prices on covers which may differ from those advertised in the text or elsewhere.

**NOT FOR SALE IN CANADA*

STAR BOOKS BESTSELLERS

CHILLERS

COME THE NIGHT	Nick Blake	£1.95
SHADOWS	Shaun Hutson	£2.25
SLUGS	Shaun Hutson	£1.95
SPAWN	Shaun Hutson	£1.80
EREBUS	Shaun Hutson	£2.25
SLIMER	Harry Adam Knight	£1.80
THE PARIAH	Graham Masterton	£2.25*
THE PLAGUE	Graham Masterton	£1.80*
THE SPHINX	Graham Masterton	£1.50*
THE DJINN	Graham Masterton	£1.50*
THE MANITOU	Graham Masterton	£1.50*
THE DONORS	Horvitz & Gerhard	£1.95*
THE SENTINEL	Jeffrey Konvitz	£1.65*
HALLOWEEN III	Jack Martin	£1.80*

STAR Books are obtainable from many booksellers and newsagents. If you have any difficulty tick the titles you want and fill in the form below.

Name ____

Address ______________________________________

Send to: Star Books Cash Sales, P.O. Box 11, Falmouth, Cornwall, TR10 9EN.

Please send a cheque or postal order to the value of the cover price plus: UK: 55p for the first book, 22p for the second book and 14p for each additional book ordered to the maximum charge of £1.75.

BFPO and EIRE: 55p for the first book, 22p for the second book, 14p per copy for the next 7 books, thereafter 8p per book.

OVERSEAS: £1.00 for the first book and 25p per copy for each additional book.

While every effort is made to keep prices low, it is sometimes necessary to increase prices at short notice. Star Books reserve the right to show new retail prices on covers which may differ from those advertised in the text or elsewhere.

**NOT FOR SALE IN CANADA*